THE RAZING

of

Voices from the American Revolution

MICHAEL S. ADELBERG

Charleston   London

THE
History
PRESS

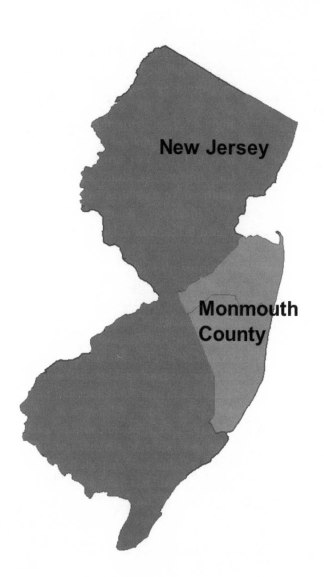

New Jersey

Monmouth
County

The Local Place Names in *The Razing of Tinton Falls*

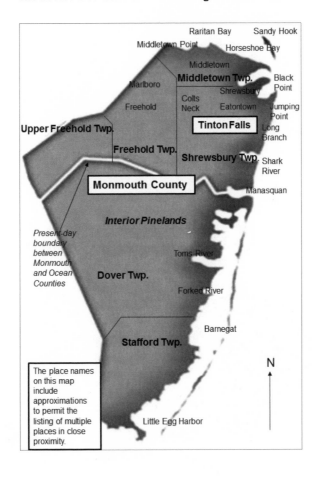

Raritan Bay

Sandy Hook

Middletown Point

Horseshoe Bay

Middletown

Middletown Twp.

Black Point

Shrewsbury

Marlboro

Colts Neck

Eatontown

Jumping Point

Freehold

Tinton Falls

Long Branch

Upper Freehold Twp.

Freehold Twp.

Shrewsbury Twp.

Shark River

Monmouth County

Manasquan

Interior Pinelands

Present-day boundary between Monmouth and Ocean Counties

Toms River

Dover Twp.

Forked River

Barnegat

Stafford Twp.

N

The place names on this map include approximations to permit the listing of multiple places in close proximity.

Little Egg Harbor

Published by The History Press
Charleston, SC 29403
www.historypress.net

Front cover painting by Linda Griggs

First published 2012

Manufactured in the United States

ISBN 978.1.60949.433.9

Library of Congress Cataloging-in-Publication Data

Adelberg, Michael, 1967-
The razing of Tinton Falls : voices from the American Revolution / Michael
Adelberg.
p. cm.
ISBN 978-1-60949-433-9
1. New Jersey--History--Revolution, 1775-1783--Fiction. I. Title.
PS3601.D4666R39 2012
813'.6--dc23
2012008742

CONTENTS

PREFACE

After publishing my history book, *The American Revolution in Monmouth County: The Theatre of Spoil and Destruction*, in the fall of 2010, the folks at The History Press asked me to consider writing a second book for them. We discussed several concepts. There was nothing wrong with any of them, but they did not excite me. With the help of Whitney Tarella, commissioning editor at The History Press, a book concept emerged that piqued my interest.

I would write a narrative nonfiction book that would seek to combine the best elements of two wonderful works: Shelby Foote's *Shiloh* (a bird's-eye exploration of a military event concurrently narrated by different participants) and Erik Larson's *The Devil in the White City* (well-researched narrative nonfiction with some fictionalization to flesh out the people and plot). I would use these two books as templates but apply them to a particular Revolutionary War event. I didn't want to write about a great battle fought by big armies but was drawn toward examining a smaller clash fought between Americans, Revolutionaries versus Loyalists.

After digging through my twenty years of research on the American Revolution in central New Jersey, I came upon the ideal event. The book would focus on a June 10, 1779 Loyalist raid against the village of Tinton Falls. The documentation of this raid was remarkably good, at least in comparison to the region's other smaller raids and clashes. Moreover, the June 10 raid had important ramifications. It was the first raid into Monmouth County motivated more by revenge than a military objective, and it started a cycle of retaliatory raid warfare back and forth across enemy lines. Additionally, the Tinton Falls raid was so effective that supporters of Revolution abandoned the village afterward.

Using my seven-thousand-person *Biographical File*, I found ten people from the Tinton Falls area—spirited Revolutionaries and avowed Loyalists, calculating opportunists and conscientious neutrals—each of whom had a dramatically different experience during the raid. I further researched genealogies and tax records to better understand these ten people, particularly their families and their economic positions. And then I began drafting *The Razing of Tinton Falls*—three nonfiction essays and ten fictionalized, intertwined narratives built from the lives of real people.

If *The Razing of Tinton Falls* succeeds in combining the best elements of *Shiloh* and *The Devil in the White City*, it is because of the great assistance received from an excellent group of editors and historians. Sally Ketchum, Tom Miglino, Whitney Tarella and Judy Adelberg (my mother) read every word of the manuscript and provided invaluable suggestions on everything from narrative voice to grammar. Five excellent historians—Todd Braisted, John Fabiano, Dave Fowler, Don Hagist and Bernadette Rogoff—reviewed the manuscript and offered excellent technical guidance on Revolutionary War military conventions, eighteenth-century material culture and biographical details of the people who appear throughout the book. They generously shared their expertise and never missed a deadline. I owe them my deepest thanks.

BACKGROUND

The American Revolution was much more than a war between George Washington's Continental army and the red-coated British. Parallel to the war between the armies, local groups waged their own civil wars. They allied themselves with one army or the other but initiated their own activities and developed their own tactics based on local conditions.

One of the most intense local civil wars was fought along New Jersey's shoreline, primarily in Monmouth County. Here, roughly twelve thousand individuals divided allegiance nearly evenly between Revolutionaries (people who supported independence) and Loyalists (people who supported continued British rule). Throughout 1776, groups of armed Revolutionaries and Loyalists arrested one another and confiscated one another's property—particularly guns, horses and wagons. In early 1777, the Revolutionaries, assisted by Continental soldiers from Pennsylvania and Delaware, broke up the organized Loyalist associations inside Monmouth County. The more devoted Loyalists fled to the British naval base on Sandy Hook (a narrow point of land at the northeast tip of the county). From there and nearby British-held Staten Island, these Loyalist refugees reorganized. For plunder and revenge, they began raiding their former home county—with the covert assistance of Loyalist sympathizers called "the disaffected" and Loyalist partisan gangs called "Pine Robbers."

A military frontier split Monmouth County between Sandy Hook and the inland regions loyal to the Continental cause. In the belt of land in between, Revolutionaries fled or laid low; Loyalist sympathizers held sway. But as the war progressed, Revolutionaries gradually reestablished order. By early 1779, these efforts included reorganizing the militia and establishing an arms magazine in the village of Tinton Falls. The Continental army supported the effort by headquartering a regiment of soldiers in the village. The Revolutionary leaders who fled at the beginning of the war—including Colonel Daniel Hendrickson, the senior militia officer for the northeast part of county—returned home. Nonetheless, Tinton Falls remained within easy reach of a determined raiding party.

On April 25, seven hundred Loyalists and British regulars marched on Tinton Falls. The purpose of the attack was to capture Colonel Benjamin Ford's Continental army regiment. But the Continentals, on first news of the British/Loyalist landing, retreated inland, leaving the local militia to offer what little resistance it could. The Loyalists looted Tinton Falls and burned the Continentals' munitions and supplies. After the attack, George Washington pulled the Continental troops out of eastern Monmouth County, determining that they had done "rather more harm than good" by serving as an attractive target to the enemy without having the strength to resist it. The Revolutionaries of Tinton Falls were now on their own.

Angered by the attack, local Revolutionaries took revenge. In May, they confiscated and sold at public auction nearly one hundred Loyalist estates. Eager to recover losses from the raid, they petitioned the New Jersey legislature for the right to confiscate property from the disaffected equivalent to the damages inflicted by Loyalist raiders. Impatient with a state government they considered dilatory and a legal system they believed was being manipulated to "shield" the disaffected, many Revolutionaries embraced armed vigilantism.

When the Continentals withdrew from Tinton Falls on May 11, local warfare increased. On May 15, a two-hundred-man Loyalist raiding party landed and marched on nearby Middletown—but the raiders halted the attack after encountering stubborn militia resistance. Later that month, there was another raid and skirmish along the Middletown shoreline. On June 5, the Pine Robber gang of Lewis Fenton murdered militia captain Benjamin Dennis near Tinton Falls. The act was not random: Dennis was a wanted man for his role in killing Jake Fagan, the notorious Pine Robber leader, months earlier. The next day, four African American Loyalists kidnapped the local constable, Zephaniah Morris, just a few days after he purchased a confiscated Loyalist estate. Then another Loyalist party penetrated the Middletown shore for the third time in a month, where it, according to a newspaper account, "plundered several houses and carried off four or five of the inhabitants."

Recognizing the worsening situation, New Jersey governor William Livingston ordered out nine companies of militia to guard the New Jersey shore and petitioned the state legislature to raise the wages for militia called out for extended duty. The governor also proposed a plan to General Washington to use jailed Continental army deserters as a special corps to hunt down Monmouth County's Pine Robbers. When Washington did not act on the proposal, the governor ordered companies of Salem and Gloucester County militia into Monmouth County. The New Jersey Assembly passed laws on May 29 and June 9 creating four new battalions of state troops, including one commanded by Colonel Asher Holmes of Monmouth County specifically for the defense of the county. Recruiting for the new state troops began in earnest. But all of these efforts needed time to take effect.

On June 9, eighty to one hundred Loyalists gathered at Sandy Hook and finalized plans to raid Tinton Falls for the second time in six weeks. Many of these Loyalists, including two of the party's leaders, Thomas Okerson and William Gillian, were from Monmouth County. They had fled the county along with a few hundred other Monmouth Loyalists two or three years earlier. Some of these Loyalists were serving in the New Jersey Volunteers—a Loyalist military unit under British command—and were granted temporary leave to conduct the raid. Some of these Loyalists had no connection with the British military. Their ranks included some slaves who had run away from slaveholding Revolutionaries in New Jersey. They now raided in ad hoc groups to support themselves.

The expedition to Tinton Falls was delayed for a day by bad weather, and then, before dawn on the tenth, the Loyalists departed. They reached the outskirts of Tinton Falls and marched on the Falls shortly after sunrise.

Upon reaching the village, the raiders split into small parties and surrounded the houses of the village's leading Revolutionaries: Colonel Daniel Hendrickson, Lieutenant Colonel Aucke Wikoff, Major Hendrick Van Brunt, Captain Richard McKnight and Captain Thomas Chadwick. The raiders achieved near total surprise; the village leaders were captured without serious opposition.

The raiders then spent the morning on the farms around the village, gathering sheep, cattle and horses (one report suggests they took three hundred head of livestock, though this is probably exaggerated). They also destroyed the arms magazine maintained for the militia at Colonel Hendrickson's barn. Several homes and buildings were burned; stores and places of commerce were looted. Benjamin White, a storekeeper at Tinton Falls, later wrote that the raiders "behaved like wild or mad men" as they went about their plundering.

Local militia harassed the Loyalists. According to a report, one militia party attacked the Loyalists "with more spirit than providence," but they were dispersed. The alarm went out for all militia and the new state troops within the county to rush to the defense of Tinton Falls. But assistance was slow to arrive from across the far-flung county. The Continentals, now gone, were missed.

In the afternoon, the Loyalists gathered up their considerable booty and left the village. They returned to the beach at Jumping Point, where their barges waited. They began the lengthy process of wading the captured livestock into the surf and onto their barges. A militia party led by Lieutenants Jeremiah Chadwick and Auke Hendrickson, both younger brothers of senior militia officers taken that morning, arrived and began firing at the Loyalists. The Loyalists returned fire, and a heated skirmish ensued. Although they were running out of ammunition, most of the militiamen stood their ground. Some Loyalists, standing exposed on the beach, used their prisoners as shields to protect themselves. Leaders among the militia and Loyalists, many of whom harbored personal grudges from earlier in the war, cursed one another. They threatened that they would grant no quarter in the event of surrender.

The Loyalists, armed with bayonets, charged the militia. They shot Lieutenant Chadwick. Fourteen militia and two Loyalists were killed in brutal hand-to-hand combat. (It is unlikely that the militia had bayonets, leaving them at a terrible disadvantage in close-in fighting.) The militia finally scattered, and the Loyalists resumed loading their booty, but much of their livestock was lost during the mêlée. After some negotiation, the militia was allowed to retrieve its wounded and dead in exchange for the Loyalists receiving no further harassment. The Loyalists escaped to Sandy Hook with their high-ranking prisoners.

The razing of Tinton Falls on June 10, 1779, was one of hundreds of small military events during the Revolutionary War. But there can be no doubt that it was the central event in the lives of the people who participated in that day. People experienced the razing of Tinton Falls in dramatically different ways: as Loyalists, neutrals and Revolutionaries; as combatants; and as noncombatants forced by events to support one side or the other. The following pages narrate the razing of Tinton Falls from the viewpoints of ten real people:

> Esther Headon, a Loyalist sympathizer who assisted the Loyalists on their landing.
> Benjamin White, a pacifist storekeeper forced to take sides.
> Deborah Williams, a vulnerable businesswoman with a Loyalist husband.
> Richard Laird, a radical militiaman from the inland village of Colts Neck.
> Mary Taylor, the daughter of a Loyalist and newlywed to a Continental soldier.

Sip, an African American Loyalist battling both the Revolutionaries and racism.

James Hulse, a reluctant militiaman with a family in harm's way.

Sarah Chadwick, a child who witnessed her father's capture.

Thomas Okerson, a young dandy and co-leader of the Loyalist raiders.

Jeremiah Chadwick, a militia officer who counterattacked the Loyalists.

These accounts and many of the details about these people are fictionalized. However, all ten of these people were real, and their narratives of June 10, 1779, are written with as much fidelity to fact as the incomplete historical record will permit. An essay at the conclusion of this book further explores the line between fact and fiction in *The Razing of Tinton Falls*.

ESTHER HEADON

Disaffected

There were many people who opposed the American Revolution in subtle ways. Some concealed their convictions, laid low and quietly supported the active Loyalists. The Revolutionaries called these covert Loyalists "the disaffected." The disaffected quietly supported Loyalist raiding parties by providing safe houses and intelligence. They also illegally traded provisions with British-held Sandy Hook and New York; this activity was so prolific that locals jokingly called it the "London Trade." In Monmouth County, the disaffected were such a problem that in 1778 and 1779 George Washington and the Continental Congress deployed a succession of Continental detachments to curb them (without much success). Though the disaffected did not take up arms, they faced significant punishments when exposed. Dozens were arrested and had property confiscated; some were beaten and killed.

At the outset of the American Revolution, Esther Frost was a widow living modestly in Middletown Township. We know she supported the Loyalists because she was indicted twice by the county's highest court, the one charged with considering war-related crimes. In 1779, Frost married Marcus Headon, whose disaffection for the Revolution equaled hers—he had three indictments before the county's highest court. It is very likely that the Headons participated in the London Trade and supported the Loyalist raiding parties that attacked Monmouth County. Between 1778 and 1784, while most of their Middletown neighbors were losing livestock to Loyalist raiders, Marcus and Esther's *livestock increased from three to eight head. The Frost and Headon surnames were uncommon in Monmouth County, suggesting that neither Esther nor Marcus had extensive family in Monmouth County. Since these family names were more common in New York, it is likely that they had family ties to Loyalists living behind enemy lines.*

To keep from sleeping more than a few hours, I didn't go to bed with Marcus last night. Instead, I slept upright in the Windsor chair with my head propped against the wall. My neck was sore, and it was pitch-dark when I awoke.

The only light came from the distant tallow candle flickering on the pewter candlestick in the front room. I took the candle and lit the lamp. I walked outside. It would be two hours until the cocks awoke and roused the farm. I was delighted by the warmth and light-blocking cloud cover: signs of providence.

Marcus had warned me that today's work would be difficult and dangerous. Captain Smock's dragoons now patrolled at night and had built beacons up and down the shore so they could respond faster to alarms. There were new state troops, mustered at Freehold and recently posted at the Falls and Shrewsbury to put a stop to the trade with New York. The confiscation of Hendrick Brewer's flour three weeks ago and the hideous murder of James Pew while in the cellar of the county courthouse last year proved that London Trading was risky business. But this was the path God had chosen for Marcus and me.

I went back inside and brought the lamp up close to the clock in the kitchen. It confirmed what I already knew: it was 3:00 a.m. I woke up Marcus by rubbing his exposed shoulders. "Marcus, time to rise, ol' man. Today's an excursion day."

I pulled on Marcus's old boots. My feet swam inside them, but the high boots kept them dry in the shin-high mud. I left the house again. I knew Marcus would be gone before my return.

Outside again, I placed cheesecloth over the lamp to dim it. It now glowed more than it lighted. I knew the path to Conkaskunk Creek well, having performed my business at night many times in the last year (was this the fifth or sixth time?). The path down to the creek was steep and often slippery, but this morning the ground was sturdy. A light wind rustled in the high grass that surrounded the path. Some of the rushes were taller than me. As I came upon the creek clearing, I heard something large jump into the water. Startled, I yelped a little. I could not see it—probably a raccoon. I wished that Marcus was with me, but I knew he was needed elsewhere.

I reminded myself that I had done this all before without him, and in the cold and rain. Today's business would be easy in comparison with the morning last March when I slipped on a lingering patch of snow, tumbled down the hill and sprained my ankle. Or last November's excursion day, when I split open my thumb while hammering through the caked-up ice on the chest that held the lamps.

I placed my lamp on the ground and removed the cheesecloth. The clearing was now well lit. I went into the meadow grass—ankle-deep in muck, shin-deep in one spot. I grasped the top of Marcus's boot to keep it from being pulled off by the sucking mud. I found the old blanket chest near the crooked cedar tree, exactly where Marcus said he had left it. I opened the chest and removed, two at a time, six tallow lamps. I put two of them in the clearing to fully light the landing point. I then walked halfway up the path and placed another lamp on the rise to light the creek bank. At the top of the hill, I placed yet another lamp. Over the crest of the hill, I placed the fifth lamp. Finally, down in the gully, near the old lean-to where two wagons waited, I placed the sixth lamp.

I went back up the hill to the barn next to the house and took out our two horses—King Herod and Esau. I led them back down the path. Esau, a strong horse as belligerent as his biblical namesake, bit King Herod in the butt, causing King Herod to whinny loudly. I felt a shiver of terror and spun my head around in the dark, silent night. Then I reminded myself that there was no one except Marcus within earshot. I hitched each horse to a wagon and quickly left the lean-to.

By the time I returned home, the horizon was orange, and Marcus was gone. There was nothing to do now but tend the house and wait.

About an hour later, at sunrise, I heard the shots go off. Marcus had fired his two muskets from the bay shore a mile away and would now be setting off in his shallop. Soon, Captain Smock's men would turn out on shore, just in time to see Marcus sailing away toward Sandy Hook.

Marcus had loaded the shallop with some hams and split wood purchased from Daniel Ketchum with no questions asked. As long as he was playing decoy on the water, he might as well conduct some trade with the king's commissary. Prices were always good on Sandy Hook, and the spring waters washing into the bay ensured that there would be no accidental grounding. But making it back home this evening would be dangerous because the militia and state troops would be out.

Reliably, within minutes of Marcus's shots being fired, I heard the signal cannon fire at Captain Smock's house to the west. The Middletown militia was on its way to the bay shore. A half hour later, King Herod whinnied loudly again. I took this as proof that the Loyalists had arrived in the creek, made their way to the lean-to and were taking the wagons. I paused and quietly prayed, wishing the Loyalists and Marcus Godspeed on the day's business.

The day was exceedingly warm, and my neck hurt from sleeping awkwardly the night before. At forty-seven years of age, I was not a young woman anymore. I thought to myself that partisan warfare was best left for young people—not graying women like me. But Marcus always reminded me that God had fated us—two childless Loyalists in our forties—to serve the king, whatever the inconvenience. And God had rightly rewarded us for our Loyalty with extra coin in our pocketbook.

I made breakfast and performed the routine farm chores. About 9:00 a.m., I stopped briefly to listen to the shooting in the distance. Marcus had told me something about what would be happening today. A party of Loyalists serving in the British army would leave Sandy Hook and land at the mouth of the Shrewsbury

River. A party of Will Gillian's refugees—also Loyalists but not in uniform—would land on the Conkaskunk Creek and pick up Marcus's wagons. They were going to meet a mile above the Falls and advance on the town, where they would relieve Colonels Hendrickson and Wikoff of their ill-gotten wealth and set fire to the rebel magazine. During the action, Marcus and the Loyalist refugees would impress the goods of the most obnoxious rebels who had harassed peaceful Loyalists for the last three years. I heard a few more scattered shots and knew that the day's business had begun.

I hoped that the musket fire did not involve Will Gillian's refugees. Marcus and Will had been friends for twenty years. As young men, they fished the banks off Sandy Hook together and took their catch to market in New York. When the war started, Will was savagely persecuted by the rebels for talking harshly about their Congress. Then Colonel Hendrickson stole Will's boat, under the pretense that Will had broken the law for visiting his sick father on Staten Island. The rebels brought Will before one of their mock tribunals and humiliated him. While Will was confined, a gang of them stole his gun, horse and wagon.

Will vowed revenge and went behind British lines. That was two years ago. Since then, he's slipped back into the creek a half dozen times at night to visit with Marcus. They would stay up all night, drinking and discussing news of the war. On each of his trips, Will brought a pouch of Continental money, but the ink on the bills ran when it rained, so we knew it was counterfeit. We kept the money dry and loaded Will's whaleboat with flour, hams or whatever else might fetch a good price in New York. A year ago, Will and Marcus struck a deal. Marcus and I would provide Will's men with a nighttime landing point and two wagons. Will would leave us a small case of money on each trip. This allowed us to serve God and the king in a more meaningful way and prosper all at the same time. I was scared and opposed the arrangement at first, but Marcus insisted that God would protect us.

Marcus and I understood the risks: if we were discovered, we might face the same mob of Presbyterian ruffians that had killed James Pew last year, or we might face arrest and the confiscation of whatever Magistrate Schenck arbitrarily declared contraband. The rebels were an awful lot. I still had nightmares from when they abused me a year ago. Like a thief or fornicator, they forced me to sleep for three nights on bare wood boards in a cell underneath the courthouse. They charged me with concealing Colonel Taylor's Loyalist militia when all I had done was provide food to four hungry men one evening. I was humiliated in court, forced to confess my loyalty to their perverse Congress and Constitution and fined £20—the value of two good horses. Fortunately, Marcus was allowed to pay the fine in their worthless currency, and they had to let me go.

We married soon after but had to drive all the way to Shrewsbury to marry amongst the Anglicans. The timorous Abel Morgan, my minister for more than ten years, now refused to marry people whom the rebels termed "disaffected." Curses on him. He used to say that only people who served God would become wealthy. Well, by his test, Marcus and I were on a godly path, while the "saints" who remained in his Baptist congregation were losing their horses and slaves.

Today's excursion was not going to be a large one like last April's. On that day, about three hundred Loyalists landed at the mouth of the creek, and three hundred British regulars landed near Shrewsbury. They met at the Falls and seized the magazine assembled there. A filthy collection of Virginian vagabonds—indolent farm hands and sailors who called themselves soldiers—were camped at the Falls. But they retreated on the first report of the landing and abandoned the rebels. A few weeks later, the Virginians left for good; not even the rebels were sad to see them go.

Today's business would be much the same, but in miniature. This time, Will would land his party of refugees in the creek. Marcus told me that Will was heading inland only to distribute General Clinton's newest declaration of amnesty, but I knew better. I knew Will would be visiting the farms of different rebels and impressing livestock. Food was scarce for the Loyalists in New York, and I knew the impressments were necessary. I hoped Will's men would not plunder personal goods or resort to violence, but so many of Will's men had been so badly abused by the rebels that they were sometimes difficult to govern—particularly the Negroes among them.

At mid-afternoon, I paused. I heard more shots. The shots went off in spurts for almost an hour. This was a bad sign; it meant that the rebel militia was making a stand against the Loyalists. To the south, I saw a thick, gray cloud of smoke rising over the trees. I shivered at the realization that the Loyalists had put the torch to Tinton Falls.

The Falls were home to terrible, abusive men like Colonel Hendrickson, Lieutenant Colonel Wikoff and the hideous Lieutenant Chadwick, who pulled Marcus out of a tavern a year ago and beat him. But they were also home to good people and inoffensive Quakers. I thought about Benjamin White, the storekeeper who continues to address me as "Good Lady" even after the rebel courts humiliated me and never casts a suspicious eye when I present the Continental money from New York. I have gone to market at the Falls for twenty years. War is nasty business—I know this even without Marcus telling me so. But when I saw the smoke cloud rising from the south, I wept like a little child for near on an hour.

At dusk comes a crashing of thunder and a brief shower, common this time of year and an appropriate ending for a day like this. With the first stretch of humid spring weather come storms like this, as well as gnats and mosquitoes. When the rebels broke our windows two years ago, swarms of insects came into the kitchen in May and never thinned until the first frost of October. We didn't have the money to buy glass for our broken windows or hire a carpenter to secure us a proper door that closed flush. Now, I stood in the kitchen and admired its cleanliness. There was barely a bug in the house. Our house was small, only two rooms and a loft upstairs, but the addition of proper windows and a good Dutch door—to say nothing of the new pewter plates and our first clock—were signs of God's providence. These were the just rewards for remaining loyal to our king while so many around us had lost their minds.

We had never farmed more than a third of Marcus's 110 acres—much of it salt marsh not suitable for crops. But this year, for the first time, we had the money to hire the old Negro Ump to help us in the fields and plow thirty additional acres. Our chances of making some real money on corn and flour this August are excellent.

I hate being alone at night without Marcus. When I'm alone, I think about my two sisters in Flatbush in Brooklyn and the cruel prohibitions the rebels placed on my going to New York. I think about my isolation and vulnerability. What if a party of drunken soldiers came to our house and found only an old loyal woman? What if a mob of Freehold Presbyterians come upon our house?

But the isolation of our house on the Conkaskunk Creek offers a strange security. We are not close to any clustering of rebels or near any of their roads. Outside of my periodic trips to Shrewsbury and the Falls, we have no contact with them. We have not attended the Baptist meeting in Middletown for two years and no longer attend the Anglican Christ Church at Shrewsbury. Marcus stays away from the Middletown town meeting and the sham elections at Freehold. Though we reap no benefit, Marcus makes it a point to pay his annual state tax at the collector's home so the collector need not come to us. If the collector saw our new door and windows and our new sows and milk cow, it would raise dangerous questions. Our isolation is our security.

When the war is over and the rebels are properly jailed, Marcus and I will have enough money to buy an excellent home near my sisters in Brooklyn. We will be the envy of our families in New York. That will make the risks we have taken well worth it.

I lie awake in bed until about midnight, when I hear the door open. It has to be Marcus, but I hold my breath waiting for confirmation. "Esther," he whispers, "Are you awake?"

I jump from the bed and light the new pewter wall sconce in the kitchen. We embrace. I pull some bread out of the Dutch oven and take a ladle of stew from the hearth pot. He shows me a thick wad of Continental money and an envelope with—oh, joy—tea leaves in it. We confess our love for each other.

For the first time since waking up twenty-one hours ago, I allow myself to feel tired.

BENJAMIN WHITE

Pacifist

The American Revolution was especially hard on Quakers. Their pacifism placed them at odds with a Revolutionary government committed to winning a war through mandatory militia service. Thousands of Quakers were fined for refusing to serve in the military or imprisoned for refusing oaths of allegiance to the United States (strict Quakers held that oaths were holy agreements with God, not government). Some Quakers loosened their religious convictions enough to pick up arms and take loyalty oaths; others became so disenchanted with what they saw as persecution that they became Loyalists. Most Quakers stayed home and did their best not to offend anyone—paying fines when required and living as normal lives as the hard times allowed. But their pacifism did not earn them protection from Loyalist raiding parties.

Benjamin White was a storekeeper at Tinton Falls. Like many Quakers, he refused to serve in the militia and was fined for delinquency at least twice. He also visited New York, even after the Revolutionary government banned such travel. Despite his troubles with the new government, White was no Loyalist. He paid his taxes, accepted Continental money (even as its value depreciated rapidly) and helped supply the French navy when it landed in American waters. He also quartered Continental troops, something many of his neighbors were reluctant to do. The decision to quarter Continental soldiers might have prompted harsh treatment from the Loyalists when they raided Tinton Falls. At war's end, in 1784, White was listed in the tax rolls as a "householder" (a person owning no

*appreciable amount of land) with no livestock. His wealth had deteriorated far
beneath the level of a prosperous storeowner.*

B enjamin White is a friend to everybody in the world." That is
what I say every morning, staring into my little shaving mirror.

"Benjamin White is a friend to everybody in the world," I hum,
sliding into my white day shirt and removing my white bib apron from
the coat hook.

Just a month ago, my apron was gray from spending each night
on the clay floor of the cellar, while my coat hook held an officer's
jacket. When Colonel Ford's Virginians came to town, I offered
my room to a red-haired captain with a fondness for drink and
a foul mouth. He proceeded to move his articles into my room
and place mine on the floor without so much as a thank-you.
He'd drink long into the night and then belch and fart through
his fitful sleep.

Sometimes, it is hard to be a friend to everybody in the world.

This became even truer when this captain led his men away from
the Falls last April on first word that the king's men had landed.
The families of Tinton Falls boarded these Virginians—and
Pennsylvanians and Marylanders before them—for six months on
the proposition that the soldiers ensured our safety. Even for a man
of peace like me, it was sickening to see the soldiers melt away in the
face of danger and leave the near-defenseless townspeople to face
the armed Loyalists.

When the captain returned, I found his company so objectionable
that I exiled myself to the cellar. It was damp and cold down there
during the rainy spring. The clay floor chilled my feet and dirtied my
clothes. But it was still preferable to being in that man's company.
Even the most hotheaded rebels like Aucke Wikoff and Thomas
Chadwick smiled when the Virginians left.

I came down the stairs into the little kitchen that sat in the back of
the store. Britton White, my older cousin and co-owner of the store
with me, was already there. He had fixed our standard breakfast:

a porridge of different grains, milk, egg and a few thin slices of salted pork. Blueberries and strawberries were now coming in, and we always pinched a few from the baskets we bought and sold. With only a 10 percent markup, no one could take issue if a few of the berries ended up in our bellies.

As merchants, we have regular access to salt and sugar—and sometimes even ginger and cloves—but we live parsimonious lives and do not indulge ourselves with exotic flavors. We sell all goods for a fair price and, when we've had a good month, use the money to make an extra mortgage payment to Aucke Wikoff. We hope to own our store outright in five years.

Britton and I exchanged our usual "G'mornings" and discussed the affairs of the day. Britton told me of a ship that had arrived from the Caribbean: "She's said to be returning from Martinique bound for Boston. She had drawn fire from a British frigate and stood into Toms River to escape capture. But she grounded in the channel and then listed onto her side in last week's storm, losing much of her cargo."

Britton would take our wagon to Toms River and see what could be purchased from the salvaged wreck. We have a friendly relationship with the village's port marshal, under whom I labored while erecting a saltworks back in 1776. If all went well, he had saved us some rum, molasses or sugar, and Britton would return tomorrow night with a full wagon. Our store was out of all drink except local apple spirits and a last bottle of Madeira wine. We were nearly out of molasses as well.

"Don't spend more than £25 for a hogshead, my dear cousin. We cannot have another predicament where we must sell rum for more than the country people can pay." This was my standard caution to Britton. Two years ago, he let a fast-talking Baltimore merchant convince him that the British blockade would never let another barrel of rum reach America—so Britton paid double market value for the merchant's rum. But the blockade has been in tatters for eighteen months now, and we are getting more Caribbean goods than any time since 1776. That was the only time Britton was swindled. Generally, he was a wise and prudent buyer—one mistake in three years was proof enough of that.

Feigning offense at my caution, Britton abruptly stood up. He jiggled the table, and it dropped his favorite wood breakfast plate to the floor. The old plate split in two. Always superstitious, Britton said, "That's a bad omen, cousin. That plate foretells one of our wagon wheels hitting a rut on the road to Toms River and splitting apart."

"No, Britton, it represents the fine wood barn of Colonel Hendrickson being split apart by ruffians from New York." I often kidded Britton for his superstitions by making dire predictions that made his seem inconsequential. Using my boot, I steered the plate pieces into the hearth. "No bad luck today, dear cousin, just kindling."

Britton grinned and left the store. I heard the wagon squeak forward. He was off for the shore before the clock hit seven chimes. With him gone, I set about cleaning the store. The farmers never came before 10:00 a.m., and I looked forward to setting out the handsome wax candles—so much better than tallow—that we purchased yesterday. I found two Continental money notes lying on the floor. The notes were for two dollars each, which could have purchased a colt in 1776 but now could barely purchase a dozen eggs.

Nobody wants the Continental notes anymore, but Britton and I know that any store in the same town as Aucke Wikoff and Thomas Chadwick better take them, whatever the discount. A silversmith in Shrewsbury refused Aucke Wikoff's Continental dollars last year; his best horse was found with a shattered leg the next morning.

About 7:30 a.m., I heard some shouts from up the street, where Colonel Hendrickson and Major Van Brunt had two of the town's finest homes. I walked onto the porch to see about the excitement, and my neck hairs stood up. Parties of armed men were at both houses. A wagon in front of Colonel Hendrickson's house held a man I assumed to be Major Van Brunt and a heavy man in his nightshirt, whom I assumed to be Colonel Hendrickson.

The king's men had somehow eluded the militia and were in town without so much as a warning shot. The countryside was not alarmed.

I shuttered the store windows and ran inside. From inside, I couldn't see anything going on in front of the store but listened as the shouting came closer. I closed my eyes and prayed: "God, thank you for taking my family to safety in Squankom, and thank you for giving Britton the wisdom to put his family there also. And thank you, God, for getting Britton out of this town today. And please, God, protect the good people of this town today, and perhaps you will see fit to protect me and this store as well."

There were several footsteps on the porch of the store. A man called to them from a distance: "It's a Quaker store. No rebels and no spirits. Move on." And they did. I thanked God for informing the men about my peaceful ways and for misinforming them regarding my trade in spirits.

Shouts continued up and down the street for the next hour. Then gunfire started. I heard a drum and commands of "form up." I heard a column of men march past the store. I put my ear to the door, and it vibrated. From a window on the side of the house, I saw perhaps thirty of the king's men in their red and green coats march toward the gunfire.

At the edge of town, near Eaton's Creek, the king's men fired a few volleys. I imagined the militia fifty feet beyond them firing back. Smoke filled the air, making it hard to see anything but the bright coats of the king's men. But I heard them shout, "Charge bayonets!" And soon they were down the street beyond Okerson's mansion, now Chadwick's farm, and out of my line of sight.

All went quiet. The king's men were gone, and the gunfire ceased. But the smoke grew thicker. A terrible thought went through my brain.

I raced out of the back door and looked back up the street. Okerson's mansion was on fire. I looked down the street and saw that the house and barn of Colonel Hendrickson were also on fire. Booms and sparks flew from the barn as stores of gunpowder and cartridges were lit by the flames. Beyond that, Lieutenant Colonel Wikoff's house and Major Van Brunt's barn were also burning.

The women and children of each family scrambled around, rescuing what they could. Panicked horses whinnied in the distance and throttled at their reins. Though the men of these Dutch families had sometimes persecuted honest Friends like me since the war began, God directed me to help. I am a friend to everybody in the world.

I ran to the Van Brunt house and grabbed the shovel from their nine-year-old lad. For the next thirty minutes, I dug furiously alongside their two male slaves. We dug a three-foot berm between the house and the fired barn. As long as the wind behaved, this barrier would protect the house. The heat from the burning barn roasted my skin. Smoke filled my nose and eyes. Sweat poured off my body. The Van Brunt daughters rushed forward with buckets of water. I drank from the same ladle as the black men without a care; even old Nicholas Van Brunt, fifty-nine and a slave owner his entire life, shared a ladle with his slaves. Britton and I—indeed, all the men of the Friends Meeting—had long tried to persuade the Dutchmen to free their slaves without success. Perhaps the Van Brunt family would remember the bravery of their slaves on this day, digging away in the shadow of a fired barn that might have killed them if it came crashing down.

When the berm was judged good enough, I ran across to the Hendricksons' and spoke to Janntje, wife of the colonel. She told me as she wept, "The savages have carried off Daniel and Daniel Jr. When little Hendrick, only nine, took a knife and stuck it into the thigh of one of their sergeants, the man said we had attacked a king's soldier and were no longer entitled to protection. Their officer walked off. The Tories then carried out all of our silver, took torches from our own hearth and lit our beds on fire. They held us away from the house for fifteen minutes until the fire was well underway. Then they went on their barbarous way, saying Wikoff's house would fare even worse."

Fighting back my own tears, I gave Janntje my handkerchief. "Mrs. Hendrickson, I will bring you and your family all the comforts my store can offer." I ran back toward the store.

The doors to the store had been pried open, and the candles and honeycombs that I had put out this morning were now overset. Two of the king's men lounged on the porch, dipping cups into a barrel of apple spirits and tearing at a fine ham Britton had hoped to sell for £3. I recognized one of the men—Reap Brindley. He had been a laborer in the area before the war but was mostly a ne'er-do-well. I remember him once asking us for work, but Britton turned him away. Britton said he was "a violent and low character."

Brindley spoke as I approached. "Don't rush to your gun over this one, Daniel. It's another one of those Quakers who live in the neighborhood. He may wish us harm, but he will do nothing more than ask his knave God to remove us."

My heart thumped loudly inside my chest. "I am Benjamin White, keeper of this store. You will know me as a neutral in this war who does not take up arms—a friend to everybody in the world. You men are welcome to food and drink. I only ask a receipt for what you consume."

The men laughed. Brindley looked at me. "I remember you, Whitey. You and your cousin were so high and mighty that you turned me away when I needed work. Now, the staff is in my hands. I think you will leave us alone or some terrible things might happen to this fine store of yours."

"I have done nothing wrong, and the king's men have orders to respect the property of neutrals. Again, all I ask is a receipt for the ham and spirits. I will appeal to your officer if I must."

On that, Brindley flew out of his chair and landed a step from me. He shoved my face and pushed me until I stumbled backward and landed on my butt. He stood over me with a knife.

"No, White, you are no neutral. I have good information that you boarded a rebel officer—an act of support for the rebel cause that proves you're no friend of our king. Now get out of here before I pull you by your starched white collar in front of Lieutenant Okerson as a rebel prisoner. You'll die on the prison ships in two weeks. Be gone now!"

I backed off and watched helplessly as the two men opened three barrels of apple spirits, filled up their canteens, took a few drinks and then kicked the barrels over. The spirits drained over the floor inside the store. Then Brindley took my broom and walked across the street to the burning Van Brunt barn. He caught the end of the broom on fire.

The smile on his face told me his evil intentions as he returned to the store. I ran up to him. "Reap Brindley, God is watching you. Don't do this!" He waved the flaming broom in my face, and I backed off. He then dropped the broom at the store entrance. A flame went up. The two men ran off laughing.

Fortunately, the floor of the store sloped a little, and most of the spirits had drained away from the entrance before the broom was dropped. With a blanket, I batted at the fire and put it out before it spread beyond the doorway.

And then I saw Brindley again, this time with my mare, Abigail. The flames and Brindley's foul ways spooked Abigail, and she made it impossible for Brindley to mount her. I went running over and put myself between the mare and Brindley. This time, when Brindley shoved me, I shoved him back. He came after me, and soon we were tussling on the ground, but I was the stronger and more sober man. My arm slid around his neck and into an unbreakable headlock. He was subdued.

Brindley snorted. "Look Whitey, my mate, Daniel, is back at your store while you're here dancing with me. I hope you stay with me the rest of the day. Daniel has always wanted to roast a sausage on the flame of a fine store like yours."

I had no choice. I let go of Brindley and went running back to the store to engage the other marauder. While climbing the stairs, I felt a hot pain in my knee. My leg gave way and crumpled beneath me. Brindley stood behind me with a wooden board. He kicked my head, and I tumbled down the steps. The two men sacked the store like wild or mad men—not even plundering, just destroying.

I crawled back behind the store to Abigail's stable. She's a good horse and calmed herself on my arrival. Though the pain was awesome, I mounted Abigail and rode her out of Tinton Falls, west toward Colt Neck.

A few miles out of town, I came upon a militia company—Colts Neck men—jogging toward the Falls. They were not too numerous, perhaps forty in all, but I thanked God nonetheless for delivering them to me.

Their captain gave me water and had one of his men set a splint for my knee. He asked me many questions about the numbers and locations of the king's men, and I answered him as best I knew. The captain then said, "We will circle south of the Falls and attack the small party at Chadwick's."

"But Captain, what about the Falls?"

"I don't have the strength to contest their main party in town. By your own report, they are too numerous. We will limit their destruction by harassing their flanks, and if we find more militia in arms, perhaps then we will retake the Falls." He then looked at me very seriously. "You must take us to Chadwick's through back paths and private fields. We cannot risk being spotted."

"Captain, I must try to save my store. I must return."

"No, storekeep, you will help us. I will arrest you and rope your hands if I must. You will guide us to Chadwick's."

And so I did. It took two hours to lead these men across deer paths and through fields to Chadwick's without going near the Falls. By the time we arrived, the Loyalists had been there and gone, and the Okerson mansion, now occupied by Captain Chadwick's family, looked like the Hendrickson's house—smoldering beams, cinders and two chimneys. Chadwick's slave was attempting to chase down the family's scattered chickens. The sight would have been comical were it not so grim.

At Chadwick's, I again implored the captain to march for the Falls. The captain again refused. Instead, he talked with his men about trying to catch the enemy at Jumping Point, three miles to the east.

His last words to me were, "Storekeeper, go home and do what you can to protect your store. Tell the people of Tinton Falls that the homes and farms of Colts Neck will be there for you in these coming days." He put a kind hand on my hand. "I wish I could do more for you."

And then he and his men jogged off toward the shore in pursuit of an enemy they likely would not catch.

Abigail brought me back to the Falls. Thank God the enemy had pulled out.

The village was an appalling mess, and the main street was littered with dry goods from my store—bags of flour, seed corn, even marl and manure. It was so senseless. Nothing created in God's image could have done such a thing unless under the control of Satan himself.

Hendrick Hendrickson, the colonel's youngest son, was at the store as I rode up. "Mother says you'll need to feed the town's suffering, Mr. White. She sent me to bring food for my family." I nodded. He went in and came out with hands full of honeycombs. Even in an emergency, the silly boy went for the sugar.

With great discomfort, I pulled myself up the stairs. I used a gun barrel, broken away from its stock, as a cane to get across the burned threshold of the store. It was dusk, and the store was a mess of overturned shelves, spills and gloomy shadows.

The boy returned with a burning twig, and we used it to light some candles and lamps. The king's men had been sloppy in their plundering, somehow leaving all of the store's glass lamps intact.

At my direction, the boy slid forward a chest of dried blackfish and the same baskets of strawberries and blueberries that Britton had pinched from this morning. We set them out for the dazed families of the village.

As for me, I took the store's lone bottle of Madeira wine and hopped back into the kitchen where this horrible day had started. I found some leftover cornbread and porridge from breakfast. My religious principles forbid me from drinking spirits, but as a young man I had broken that rule a few times—drinking with my old friend, the miller John Williams, now a Loyalist. I liked the feeling of drunkenness.

I set the pot of porridge in front of me and looked at the bottle of wine. I had not eaten since morning, and the cold porridge tasted delicious. Tears came down my cheeks as I uncorked the bottle.

Voices from the American Revolution

I stood up with the wine bottle and saw that my hands were shaking. Scanning the overturned shelves of my store, I repeated, "Benjamin White is a friend to everybody in the world." I slid the cork back in, put the wine back on a shelf and started cleaning up the store—continuing without a break until sunrise.

DEBORAH WILLIAMS

Businesswoman

Hundreds of Loyalist men left Monmouth County to join the British in New York. In many cases, their families went with them, but in other cases, the wives and children stayed home. No doubt, the husbands' decision to leave home strained relations with the left-behind spouses. For the wives who remained, the war years were hard: dozens of families with Loyalist fathers were forced off their estates when authorities seized them. But some Loyalist wives cleverly cultivated relationships with the new Revolutionary leaders and were allowed to maintain their family estates. However, clever as these women were, they were not spared the violence that accompanied civil warfare.

Before the war, Deborah Williams and her husband, John, owned a mill and lived comfortably at Eatontown, near Tinton Falls. When the war began, John became a Loyalist. He was captured and deported to faraway Frederick, Maryland. After his release, he fled behind British lines to New York and became a captain in the Loyalist New Jersey Volunteers. Deborah stayed home and managed the family mill. It appears that she became, based on fragmentary evidence, a successful businesswoman and supporter of the Revolution. But none of her adaptability mattered when a party of Loyalist bandits arrived. Before the war's end, Deborah Williams had lost the family mill (likely destroyed), lost the farm on which the mill stood and was, at least temporarily, reduced to receiving poor relief.

D ays at the mill always began the same way. Billy, my servant lad of fourteen, rapped gently on my door. "G'morning Missus Williams. Would you like to wake up now?" I never replied to Billy's question. After a few seconds, I'd hear his shoes on the stairs returning downstairs.

I opened the door. Billy had, as he always does, left a washbasin with fresh water and soap for me. I brought them inside my room. The cool water felt good on my face and chased away the lingering grogginess. The tall-case clock in the hallway began the first of seven chimes.

Looking out my bedroom window, I saw the water wheel turning at its brisk spring pace. It was early in the year for flour milling, but there was still business from last year's hoarders—mostly Dutchmen. They held wheat seed through the winter and milled it in the spring when prices were higher. "God bless the hoarders," I whispered, "for they keep the miller in business year round."

I opened the closet and fingered each of the four well-ironed dresses. Good fortune had smiled on me—so many people had nothing in these times of hardship. My hand pushed past the two brown matronly dresses, the kind favored by Quakers. I grabbed a yellow and blue silk dress as pretty as the wildflowers blooming along the Falls Road.

John frowned at me for wearing such fancy things. He had long parted ways with the Quakers but still wanted his wife plainly dressed. His opinion no longer mattered. My mind wandered as I put on the dress and thought about how John and I had also parted ways.

Like John, I was raised among the Friends. My parents were very strict, but I was fortunate to have a father who wanted his daughter to learn to read and keep numbers. When John and I married, I helped him negotiate the mortgage. John and I split and sawed wood together as we raised the mill house. It was my cousin who financed the mill's first grinding stone under very lenient terms. As John was sometimes absentminded in matters of business, I kept the mill's account book and flattered the constable into action when indebted farmers needed some "persuasion" in settling their accounts.

Twice a week at dawn, John loaded our small sloop with the mill's flour and left for New York. As the sloop was too small for even a hammock, he'd sleep on the boat, lying across the flour sacks. When the winds were harsh, he'd stay in New York or at Sandy Hook for days at a time. The loaded sloop was a death trap on rough waters, and John did not take chances. But when he returned, it was always with a wad of money and something for the family—a pewter sconce, silver shoe buckles, some ground ginger. John never squandered a single half penny on drink, evening women or games of chance. He was a sober and serious husband, a good father to our five children and the upstanding owner of the best mill in the township.

When people started talking about independence, John made enemies. He and William Taylor led a petition arguing against independence, saying it would bring a ruinous war to our peaceful and prospering colony. At the 1776 Shrewsbury town meeting in January, John protested that the British system, even with its problems, "was doubtless the best in the universe." After that, some people boycotted our mill, driving two miles around us to go to the mill at Tinton Falls, even though Hendrickson had higher rates for anyone he called disaffected. A group of boys from the Falls, the sons of Thomas Chadwick and Aucke Wikoff, broke the windows of our mill house with rocks.

John nearly went with Lieutenant Colonel Morris when sixty Loyalists marched off to join the British in July. I told John it would be madness to leave our mill just after we paid off the mortgage. Reluctantly, he stayed. But all through the fall, John helped a Loyalist group at Long Branch—bringing them flour and never asking for repayment. When their foolhardy leader, Samuel Wright, wanted to go to New York, John gave him our sloop. Wright was caught, and John was exposed as disaffected.

More people boycotted our mill, and our income dropped to near nothing. John was bitter. He told me that when the British army arrived in New Jersey, he would throw in his lot with them. He waved me off when I pleaded with him to lay low.

When the British army entered New Jersey in December, John joined it. He was commissioned as a captain in Squire Taylor's provisional government—supporting the soldiers of Lieutenant Colonel Morris. A few days later, John led a posse down the shore, through Long Branch, Manasquan and Toms River, confiscating guns, horses and wagons from the rebels. The day before Christmas, John took possession of the saltworks at Toms River and sent its Philadelphia manager fleeing into the woods. But two weeks later, Lieutenant Colonel Morris withdrew, leaving John and his posse alone. John was taken by the rebels and marched, in the middle of the winter, all the way to Frederick, Maryland. He was released into British lines three months later. Lieutenant Colonel Morris made him a captain of the Jersey Volunteers.

I didn't know any of this as it was happening. For months I heard nothing and assumed John was still jailed in Maryland. In October 1777, ten months after he disappeared, John came home. The militia was away, fighting at Germantown alongside General Washington, and Loyalists used the opportunity to cross back into New Jersey and visit family. When John showed up in a fine military uniform, I nearly fainted.

After the children went to sleep, we went outside and argued for two hours about whether the family should leave with him. When John admitted he didn't even have so much as a boardinghouse room for us, I reasoned, "We cannot give up a prosperous mill for a soldier's salary and a dismal cabin on Sandy Hook, living among the blacks."

He looked at me with angry eyes that were alien to me. "You're now an officer's wife and will take orders like an officer's wife."

I laughed. "John, this war has made you mad." I reached to touch his cheek and defuse his anger, but my hand never reached him. His punch knocked me to the ground. I spit two bloody teeth into my hand. I cursed him, ran into the house and locked the door. We have not attempted to communicate since.

To earn the favor of Colonel Hendrickson and Lieutenant Colonel Wikoff, I told everyone about my ugly incident with John. Now the rebel families call me "Widow Williams" to imply that John is dead to us. The nickname doesn't bother me.

The person in the blue dress in the mirror smiled. For a gap-toothed widow, I still looked good. My figure was round in the right way and my face unwrinkled for a woman turning forty. Vincent Wainwright, a widower and the younger brother of a militia captain, smiles at me each Sunday coming out of church. Maybe I will start smiling back. Even if he thinks my most attractive feature is a prosperous mill, it will be nice to be held by a man again. And I know enough of Vincent's character and family to know him a decent man. Yes, I will smile at Vincent at the Anglican meeting this Sunday.

I came down the broad staircase and entered the main hallway of the house. When the mill became profitable ten years ago, John and I built ourselves a proper two-story Georgian. This hallway is our jewel—with broad, stained floorboards and a doublewide front door with bull's-eye glass that casts little rainbows across the floor on sunny mornings. I looked at a pretty swirl of light at the foot of the stairs and playfully hopped over it. The children have this charming superstition that says that leaping the rainbow brings good luck. By their rules, it should have been a lucky day.

Before heading into the kitchen, I sat down briefly at my desk and scanned the numbers. Around this time of the month, I send out Billy to ask the delinquent farmers to settle their accounts. I do this in preference to alerting the magistrate, as no one wants to see these people fall in line as bad debtors before the court of common pleas. I wrote six names on a slip of paper and entered the kitchen.

The kitchen was full of its usual morning bustle. My four younger children—Elizabeth, Peggy, Jane and Benjamin—were at the table: three chattering girls and a put-upon little boy. My oldest, John Jr., had moved up the road to a two-room cottage near Tinton Falls with his new wife.

With John Sr. gone and now John Jr. gone, too, there's no true man in the house. Six months ago, Rebecca Dennis was viciously beaten and robbed in her house by a gang of Pine Bandits while her husband and grown son were out with the militia. They live only two miles to the south. It makes me sick thinking about my family's vulnerability—especially when every ruffian up and down the shore knows of our prosperous mill.

Each morning, Billy and Deliah tend the kitchen. Deliah, just turned fifteen, was born to a migrant woman who drank heavily and was said to be a whore. As a favor to the township's overseer of the poor, John and I took the child when she was two and have kept her ever since. I still receive a small stipend for taking care of her. Deliah turned into a wise long-term investment. Although she's a little slow in the head, she's grown into a faithful and competent house servant, the equal of a good slave. At eighteen, her bond will be done, and I'll help her find a landowning husband who will not hit her.

Our good fortune was equaled with Billy. John found Billy on the docks of New York five years ago. He was nine and had come across the Atlantic from Ireland as a stowaway. Billy latched onto John and became his boat hand. When John became involved in the war, he told Billy to stay home and help me at the mill. Billy now lives with the family as a servant without a legal indenture. We treat him well, and he stays willingly. Life in our house is doubtless far better than anything he'd seen during his miserable childhood.

I was greeted by a round of "G'mornings." Deliah set out a plate for me: cornbread, peas and a handsome slab of ham. In the old days, when I was more religious, I would have broken into prayer at this evidence of prosperity. The war had been so hard on so many people, including godly people up and down the shore. Yet my family prospered, even after John left for the enemy and the Friends expelled me for not renouncing John Jr.'s service in the militia. When the Friends sent old Elihu Williams to counsel me, the last step before expulsion, I told him I supported John Jr.'s militia service because it would keep the rebels from seizing the mill. He called me a cynic, and I was expelled the next week. Even now, I consider myself true to the principles of the Friends but now attend the Anglican meeting, where everything is more lenient.

Since the Tories broke the water wheel axle at Hendrickson's mill during April's attack, every farmer from Manasquan to Tinton Falls comes to me. Now, we work day and night and still have to turn people away. I lectured John Jr. about giving everyone, from the most ardent Tory to the most fervent Rebel, the same prices and offering everyone generous terms if they cannot pay. For widows and families that have suffered, we grind their meal for free as long as they come in the evening. In exchange, I only ask that they speak of my generosity at their next church meeting.

John Jr. and I argued about this once, after he totaled the money lost. I told him, "We need the community to think that the loss of the Williams mill would be a tragedy. Goodwill is our only protection. Starving people become the brigands and robbers who sack prosperous mills."

After breakfast, Billy and I walked over to the mill. The wheel was creaking away and sat slightly off kilter. Although John Jr. disagreed, I was certain the tilt was getting worse. It would be a costly repair that would require an expert millwright. I thought about the bother of placing an ad in the Philadelphia newspapers and the expenses: boarding a millwright for a month, paying for the custom-made iron axle and spindle, repairing the waterlogged parts of the wheel and probably switching out the grinding stones. The mill would sit motionless for a month—meaning no income for the family. We'd need a sizable nest egg by winter.

Billy and I entered the mill house. It was especially noisy in the spring when the stream was fast. John Jr. had his back to us and was dumping sacks of last year's corn onto the wheel for grinding. Even without looking, I could tell he was grinding corn. Ground corn lets off a sweet, slightly burnt smell—far more pleasing to the nose than the sour, nutty smell of grasses like rye and wheat.

John didn't hear us come in. I paused to watch him. From behind, he looks just like his father at the same age: slender body, wispy brown hair thinning on top, bowlegs. He also whistles like his father—though the grinding of the wheel made it impossible to discern his tune.

He jumped with a start when he caught sight of Billy and me. "For God's sake, mother, you scared me." Then he looked at Billy. "And you are such a stealthy lad, Billy, I thought you was Jake Fagan, himself, with your sneaking ways." Stealthy or not, Billy idolized John Jr.—the big brother he never knew. Billy joined John Jr. at the millstone, scraping off cornmeal into the sacks. The two young men were dusty yellow within a few minutes.

I sat down in the corner and took out a sewing needle, repairing sacks to the loud, thumping rhythm of the mill wheel. I thought about the profits that would come from another good season. Maybe I could delay the repairs to the mill for another year. Maybe this would be the year to bring in a tutor and teach the children French and Latin. Even with their father in New York, I could make my children the equal of any squire's child in the county.

Perhaps an hour later, Deliah came running into the mill house. She shouted over the din, "Missus Williams, John…the signal cannon's fired! It's fired!"

John hurriedly dumped his sack, dusted off his shirt and walked toward the door. I stood up, "Don't go, John. Stay here. The clunking mill wheel drowned out the signal cannon. You never heard it. Deliah never said anything. Nobody could blame you for not turning out."

John shook his head and walked out.

Billy followed. At the door, he looked at me. "Missus Williams, I am fifteen now. Boys my age are turning out. John Jr. has told me I could turn out with him anytime you says I can."

"It's 'say' Billy, not 'says.' And I most definitely *say* you cannot go with John Jr. You are not of age, and I need you here. You're the man of this mill now." I walked over and kissed his sweaty, dusty forehead. "You're nearly a son to me, Billy, far more than a servant boy. Stay close. Protect the family."

He blushed. John Jr. rode off.

I sent Deliah to fetch the children from the orchard where they were picking blueberries. Soon, the children and I were putting our fowl and goats inside their pens. "No stragglers. Git, now!" they shouted above the wheezes and squawks of the unhappy animals. The goats in particular were stubborn about being put back in their pens early. Deliah shuttered the house and bolted the door as the children came inside.

Billy left with the family's two guns and perched himself in the loft of the mill house. From there he could see trouble coming up the road from Tinton Falls and guard all three of the property's important buildings: the house, the mill and the barn. During the awful raid last April, Billy had to fire warning shots to keep two deserters out of our barn. They were from Colonel Ford's Virginia Continentals, sent to Tinton Falls to protect us. While two shots from the loft might be enough to frighten off a couple of rogues, Billy had strict directions never to fire on a large party or an officer. We would not invite retaliation from a gang of riled men.

I knew the Loyalists would eventually return. April's attack had proved that the Continentals could not defend us, and Tinton Falls still harbored attractive targets for the Loyalists: the arms magazine at Colonel Hendrickson's and people like Aucke Wikoff and Thomas Chadwick, whom so many Loyalists hated.

Our house and mill sat two hundred feet from the road, up a lovely drive lined with young fruit trees. Owning a prosperous mill so close to the main road made us a likely target. People were surprised that the Loyalists had not visited my mill on their last attack, even after disabling the mill at Tinton Falls just two miles away. I said it was "God's providence" that spared us, even though I was pretty certain that it was John's influence.

There was nothing to do now but wait. I wasn't much of a church woman anymore, but I was glad when my children and Deliah gathered in a circle in the hallway to pray. The children said a prayer for John Jr.'s safety and a second prayer to be left alone from all armed men today.

We listened to the scattered gunfire in the distance.

At about 11:00 a.m., the firing stopped. It seemed like a miracle. Only days later did I learn that the firing stopped because this was when the militia broke ranks and fled. Minutes later, Billy shouted, "Loyalists...maybe a dozen, coming up the path with a wagon!"

Goose pimples ran up my arms. I called the children over. "Now remember, we are a *loyal* family, and we are delighted to see these men. Only speak when spoken to, but if spoken to, remind the men that you are the children of John Williams, a captain in the Jersey Volunteers."

I looked in the mirror and straightened my dress, "Steady, Deborah, these are the king's men, and you're an officer's faithful and suffering wife." I slid back the bolt and opened the door.

Billy called out, "Huzzah to the loyal men!" as the party entered the yard.

They were a handsome bunch: neat red and green coats over white trousers. The best dressed of them, a large man sitting in their wagon, stepped down and came toward me.

"I am Sergeant Worthly, and I am here to purchase as much ground cornmeal and flour as I can fit on this wagon. You are Mrs. Williams, wife of Captain John Williams, is that right?"

"Yes, Sergeant." I gave him a curtsy and half bow. "Thank you for allowing me to support the king's soldiers." The sergeant rolled his eyes, suggesting that he knew my gestures of loyalty were overdone. "I'm glad, Mrs. Williams, that you're not among the Loyalist wives with two strings on their bow—playing one of two tunes depending who is in the yard." He chuckled. I blushed.

Worthly motioned for two of his men to come forward. "Thank you, Mrs. Williams. These men will carry as much as we can from your fine mill. In the meantime, my men would welcome any spirits you might have. Please bring the drink to us."

"Of course, Sergeant. Deliah, Elizabeth, bring the men all the cider we have. Quickly, now!" I gave the sergeant a warm smile to convey my thanks for keeping his soldiers outdoors. Soldiers, regardless of which side they fight for, always cause mischief inside well-appointed houses.

Billy came down from the mill loft and helped the soldiers, one of whom looked no older than Billy himself. They loaded the wagon with a dozen sacks of flour and eight of cornmeal. Worthly counted the sacks twice and gave me a receipt for "24 sacks of fine flour and cornmeal." He explained, "I cannot get you compensated for the drink given my men, but I reckon four extra sacks on this receipt will make up for that. Have your boy bring the receipt to the commissary at Sandy Hook tomorrow—after the affairs of today are settled."

The sergeant tipped his hat. "And be careful, Missus. All manner of plunderer and common thief will walk these roads now that the rebels are scattered." Then they were off. I hugged each of the children and wiped the sweat from my forehead with a handkerchief. Billy asked if he needed to stand sentinel any longer.

"They've gone, Billy. No need to stand sentinel any longer. You did a fine job today."

Not even an hour later, two ragged-looking men came up the drive. Deliah spotted them first and called, "Children, inside at once! Missus Williams, Missus Williams, men are coming!"

I hurried outside as fast as I could and met the men as they entered the yard. A tall man spoke first. "This is a mighty prosp'rus mill, Missus. The king, he says that loyal men like us must rely on the gen'rus support of loyal country people like you, Missus Williams."

I didn't like that the man knew my name. Nor did I like his slurred speech. He appeared drunk.

"We will be pleased to bring food to you and your, eh, companion, sir. You can also have the run of our orchard with its young apples and blueberries. My girl will fetch any drink you desire. Please make yourselves comfortable in our yard. Deliah, Billy, bring chairs for these men."

The tall man made a waving motion and looked annoyed, "No, ma'am, we need your horses. We must have horses to catch up with the Loyalists. We wuz separated from them." He looked at Billy. "Boy, saddle up two horses, and stuff the saddle bags with food. Then we'll be on our way."

Billy froze. The man stepped toward him.

I put myself between. "Sir, we are not as comfortable as you might think—and not so comfortable that we can part with two horses, even for the king's men. We have only three horses and use them daily to bring milled grains to Sandy Hook to feed the Jersey Volunteers. Surely, you don't want to leave the lone mill in the neighborhood unable to bring flour to the loyal soldiers on Sandy Hook. My husband, *Captain* John Williams of the *Jersey Volunteers*, would not want that, nor would his longtime friend, *Colonel* John Morris. Besides, we've already contributed twenty-four sacks of grain and cornmeal to Sergeant Worthly. You can even ask him."

The tall man spit on the ground and said to his friend, "Daniel, that woman sure can talk. Giving me a headache lis'nin to her. Let's get the horses and go."

The second man walked toward the barn. As he threw the barn door open, Billy attacked him from behind with a shovel. After taking two whacks, the man wrestled the shovel out of Billy's hands. Soon, he was hitting Billy with the shovel and laughing about it.

I went running over, but the tall man tackled me from behind. "You'll stay here, Missus." He sat his large body on top of me and rubbed my face in the dirt when I tried to squirm out from under him. I coughed the dirt out of my mouth. Little mud pies formed in the dirt below as tears fell off my face.

The other man beat up Billy for another five minutes. When Billy stopped struggling, the man dragged him to a tree and roped him around it. Then the man saddled two horses in the barn and brought them out.

The tall man let go of me and started walking for the horses. Then I heard a shot fire from the house. The tall man fell, cursing and holding his leg.

Deliah stood near the porch, twenty feet away, trembling with a smoking gun. The robber left the horses and came running toward Deliah. He pulled the gun from her hands and struck her across the chest with the gunstock in a most barbarous way. She lay whimpering in front of the porch. The man returned, dragged me to the orchard and tied me around a pear tree. Then he did the same with Deliah. He returned to the wounded robber.

From a distance, I watched the two robbers argue. Then the healthy robber propped up his injured comrade and helped him into the house. I prayed that my children were well hidden. The healthy robber emerged a few minutes later with my silver candlesticks peeking out of an overstuffed sack. "Fare thee well, Reap!" He laughed and rode off.

A few minutes after the men left, Elizabeth came running toward me with a small kitchen knife. The knife did a poor job of cutting the tough hemp rope, but with persistence, the fibers frayed and I pulled my hands free. I untied Billy and Deliah in short order. Billy was a mess of welts and still in a stupor. Deliah and I half dragged him to the porch.

The children, thank God, had taken refuge in the root cellar and were unharmed. They came out when they saw us coming. We all hugged on the porch.

From inside the house, the tall man shouted, "Missus, Missus! I have two loaded guns that says I am your house guest now. Have one of the children bring me drink and some bread. I won't be no trouble to anyone long as I get proper hospitality."

"My children will not go near you, sir. You will stay in the house alone and pray for God's mercy for what you have done to an innocent and loyal family."

I turned to Deliah, "Deliah, go into the kitchen and get every knife. Then take the children and Billy and hide in the barn. Make sure each of the children have a knife, pitch fork or shovel. If that terrible man should come, you all must fight him. But I don't think he can walk, so you should be safe. I will take Parcelot and ride for help." Deliah nodded. She crouched down and ran into the kitchen.

The man shouted, "I will kill you all if you don't bring me somethin' to drink!"

I hitched up Parcelot and rode for the Falls. The road was eerily quiet, and the air smelled of smoke. The Falls were home to people who had used the Revolution to profit and raise their status in the community. Some of these people, like Lieutenant Colonel Wikoff, were arrogant and mean to families like mine. But with an adult son serving faithfully in his militia regiment and my generous contributions to the suffering families, even a greedy man like Wikoff knew he could not seize the mill. I thanked God that John Jr.

had not gone off with John and asked Him to look out for John Jr. and keep him safe.

The Falls were a horrible scene. Several of the buildings were plundered clean. Major Van Brunt's barn was on fire, and the family's slaves were furiously shoveling dirt to keep the flames from spreading to the house. Colonel Hendrickson's barn, the one that served as the township's magazine, was burned to the ground. The Loyalists had taken all of the military supplies, except three muskets that they bent around a fence post in heart shapes to mock the militia. The town's best store, maintained by the inoffensive Quakers Britton and Benjamin White, was plundered and abandoned, its contents strewn about the street.

I was astonished that the king's men could behave this way and hated John for going off to serve with men who could do this. There was no militia in sight, save a wounded young man outside White's store. His head was badly burned and scarred. I dismounted and brought him some water. He was groggy and kept calling me "Altje," a common Dutch name. I tore off the sleeve of my dress and cleaned his wound with half of it, using the rest of the sleeve for a bandage.

I continued nursing the man as a party of thirty militia came up the Falls Road. Their clean clothes suggested that they had not seen any action. I ran to the man who appeared to be their leader. "Captain, I am Deborah Williams of Eatontown. My family has suffered a brutal robbery today from two Tory robbers. My servant boy is wounded. One of the bandits remains in my house, in a lower bedroom, with my family's guns now turned against us. Please help."

The officer called back to his men, "What say we help this poor woman?" Most of the men cheered.

It was already dark when we reached the house. I rapped lightly on the barn door. "Deliah, Elizabeth, is everybody safe?" The door opened, and I was covered in warm hugs from everybody—everybody except poor Billy. He sat against a wall of the barn in a daze, a carving knife on top of his belly.

I went to him. "Poor lad, who will you stab with that knife?" He didn't even blink. The welts and wounds on his head were visible even in the dark, shadowy barn. "It is alright, my brave boy. Help is here."

The militia divided into two groups, stationed at the front and back doors. Their assault happened suddenly, and I was caught by surprise when I heard two shots in quick succession from inside the house. Then it went quiet. Soon, militiamen were filing out of the house.

It was dark, and I couldn't see the officer coming toward the barn. I was startled when he called, "Ma'am, the Tory is dead. So is one of my men. We'll need shovels and lamps to dig two graves."

Deliah led one of the militia into the mill house, and soon they had lit up the yard with several lanterns. The children brought out our four shovels. The men quickly dug two shallow graves in the orchard.

The bodies were brought out of the house. The Tory was dragged out by his feet, a slick of blood leaking from his skull. His head bounced on each porch step, making an almost hollow sound. One of the militiamen imitated the sound, and the men laughed.

"Deliah, you'd best start cleaning up inside the house. It will be a terrible mess in there." She nodded and went into the house.

I left Elizabeth with Billy, and the rest of us attended the burial.

Several of the militiamen spit and kicked the bandit's corpse as it was dragged toward the grave. My little Benjamin, just eight, ran forward. "Benjamin, get back here!" I called, but it was too late. The men cheered on little Ben as he kicked the body a half dozen more times. They dumped the body, face first, into the grave.

The slain militiaman came next. He was wrapped in a bedsheet and carried out by four men with as much dignity as possible. We all prayed quietly when the captain called out, "This will be the final resting place for the body of brave James Pearce." I never knew this man but wept for him as if he were my own son.

By 9:00 p.m., the Colts Neck militia was off, and my family returned to the house. Deliah had scrubbed the hall clean of the bandit's bloody trail, but a look into the back bedroom sickened me. The bed

was stained with blood, and there was a hole in the headboard and wall behind it where the Tory had been shot. Chunks of his innards sat on the floor next to the bed. A swarm of flies buzzed above, made giddy by their disgusting feast.

I left the room. Cleaning it would be a terrible job, and one that would wait until morning. I sent Deliah out to the barn to sleep next to Billy and brought the children upstairs.

I hope their nightmares will be milder than mine.

RICHARD LAIRD

Radical Revolutionary

Some viewed the American Revolution as a struggle for survival against an evil enemy. The powerful Loyalist raids and weak support from the state and Continental governments stoked frustrations inside Monmouth County. Monmouthers earnestly petitioned the New Jersey legislature for the right to retaliate more forcefully against their Loyalist enemies by practicing eye-for-an-eye justice against any Loyalist they might capture. Even before the razing of Tinton Falls, at least two Loyalists captured in Monmouth County were killed without trial. After the raids of 1779, a five-hundred-man armed vigilante society known as the Retaliators was founded. Over the next few years, this group carried out dozens of violent acts. The treatment of captured Loyalists in Monmouth County was a cause of great controversy until the war's end. Loyalists insisted that they were soldiers deserving of the same prisoner of war status and protections as captured British soldiers, while aggrieved local militia viewed them as pirates and murderers deserving of little or no legal protection.

The Laird family owned several farms and distilleries in Freehold and neighboring Colts Neck. Most were strong supporters of the Revolution. Richard Laird owned a small forty-five-acre farm in Freehold Township. He was one of several members of the family to join the Retaliators and sign pro-retaliation petitions. He was also a faithful militiaman, serving as a sergeant in the militia and later enlisting as a sergeant in the state troops. The men of Laird's neighborhood *were generally spirited in responding to alarms and often made long marches to the shore to battle with Loyalist raiding parties. Many of these same men were Retaliators; their urges to punish their enemies were rarely checked by their officers or legal due process.*

I was fixing the fence on the north field when I heard the signal cannon fire at Captain Smock's in Middletown. As a Freehold man, I was not bound to respond to an alarm from a neighboring town, but I knew that if the Middletown men were being roused, it was for good reason.

I turned to Richard Jr., who was holding a new rail in place, waiting for me to secure it. He's a good, obedient boy—only eleven and already more helpful than a slave. "Your father is needed by the militia today, boy. Get your sister and finish the fence." Junior opened his mouth to protest but swallowed his words when I gave him a harsh look.

I walked to the barn and started saddling my horse. Margaret, my oldest daughter, brought out my musket, powder horn and cartridge pouch. This was the fourth alarm already this spring, and Margaret cried each time. Last year, her friend's father, Leonard Hoff—a good man for an Anglican—was killed when the Tories struck at Middletown Point and burned down the storehouses. I have little patience for weak, weeping women, but I always forgive Margaret. I know she fears for my safety.

Margaret, for her part, stayed relatively composed. "Please be careful today, Father. God be with you." I kissed her forehead, and she backed away, barely containing the tears in her eyes.

Another good child. "Tell your mother I'm out on alarm. I will be back tonight. Make sure your brother saves me some ham. No crying. Now go and help your brother fix the fence. I'm counting on you. We can't have the deer eating our corn."

It was only a short ride to Widow West's tavern at Colts Neck. Officially, Colts Neck was part of Shrewsbury Township, the township known for weak-willed militia officers and men who do not fulfill their duty on alarm. But the Colts Neck men are different from the rest of their township. Most are good Presbyterians who worship with their kin in Freehold. So my captain, Kenneth Hankinson, and the Colts Neck captain, James Green, reached an understanding that as long as their men were turning out, it didn't matter whether they mustered at Captain Hankinson's distillery in Freehold or Captain Green's muster site, Widow West's tavern at Colts Neck.

I live two miles from either site but always go to the widow's tavern. This is because my cousin Robert, maker of the finest apple spirits in the county, prefers the widow to Hankinson, whose weak spirits undersell Robert's. He and the widow make sure the Colts Neck men are properly steeled for battle before we leave the tavern. The strong drinks lure me and several others to Colts Neck.

Halfway to Widow West's tavern, I heard the signal cannon fire at the courthouse in Freehold. Now it was officially my alarm, too. Riding onto the Falls Road toward Colts Neck, I met Samuel and James Pearce, my boyhood friends and relatives by marriage. Before reaching the widow's tavern, five others had joined us. Three of the men walked; they were farm laborers. One was young Tunis Van Schoick, just sixteen and barely more than one hundred pounds but already a veteran of three skirmishes with the Tories.

Widow West's tavern isn't much to look at. It's a simple four-room house with an attic instead of a second story. Besides a great room added ten years ago, the widow's tavern is no larger than an ordinary farmhouse. The cedar shingles on the house's exterior are rotting off, and the bricks in the stoop are cracked and out of alignment. The only suggestion that it is a tavern is made by a small wooden ball, painted a fading blue, that hangs from a poplar tree between the house and the Falls Road.

Lydia West is a known eccentric. She argues with the men about politics and world events. She talks of emancipating the slaves, mocks the curative powers of our local physician and boldly predicts "a day when the nations of Europe will kneel before the great United States of America." But for all her bombast, the widow runs a respectable public house. She serves fine meat pies, and because she's favored by Colonel Daniel Hendrickson, she always has current newspapers from Philadelphia—sometimes only a week past the printing date.

The widow rarely has overnight guests at her tavern, though she caused a great commotion two weeks ago when she took in the shamed Mary Taylor and her bonny Virginia groomsman. We all understand that our small coins keep the widow from becoming a ward of the overseer of the poor. James Pearce wisely observed, "We can get a full belly and some spirits for our money, or we will have to give the same money to poor relief to support the crazy old woman. And then we get nothing for it. I prefer the food and drink."

There's another reason for meeting at the widow's tavern: there's no better choice. In all Colts Neck, there are only two other buildings of any size—the competing tavern of Joshua Huddy and the store of Levi Hart. Many would prefer meeting at Huddy's tavern. It's bigger, and it has dominos and playing cards. But Huddy's ugly personal life has estranged him from the religious men in our company. Captain Green reckons that some men would use Huddy's adulterous relationship with young Lucretia Emmons as an excuse to avoid muster. The other large building is the store of the Jewish peddler Levi Hart. No one bears the son of Abraham any malice for his strange religion, but using a Jew's house as a muster site is out of the question.

By noon, I was on my fourth drink, and the militia ranks had swollen to thirty, about two-thirds of the district. The great room of the widow's tavern was full of more than people. It was an assemblage of smells: applejack, pipe tobacco and sweat filled the air, each one more pungent than the others depending on the current draft of air. Gnats and mosquitoes by the dozens came in through the open windows and door.

In some parts of the state, a turnout of two-thirds the men might be considered disappointing. But it was good by Monmouth County standards, where a third of the people are Tories and another third are trimmers whose loyalty blows with the day's fickle wind. The Presbyterian families of the district—Lairds, Pearces, Andersons and Wallings—make up most of the men of who muster reliably.

Sometimes we even jokingly call ourselves the Presbyterian Association of Colts Neck, but the captain discourages this because he says it makes the Dutchmen and Quakers feel unwelcome.

I was finishing a drink with my good friend Samuel Pearce when Captain Green arrived. "Pardon me, boys, for not making your party on time, but it appears the widow's been treating you all just fine." A round of cheers and huzzahs went up for Widow West. Because the Tories were after him, Captain Green had left his farm between Colts Neck and Tinton Falls and moved to Freehold. Now he was nearly an hour's ride away from Colts Neck. This means the captain is frequently the last man in his own company to turn out on alarm—but we all understand that as a wanted man he had to move farther inland for his safety.

Besides, the captain's tardiness allows us to carouse at Widow West's before duty, which all the men enjoy. Well, all the men except the fighting Quakers, Benjamin and James Jackson. Their religious piety keeps them from entering a tavern but still somehow allows them to carry arms. Through the revelry, the Jackson men stood outside sipping water from the widow's well and eating wild strawberries.

At first glance, Captain Green doesn't appear much of a man— he's bald, potbellied and not even five and a half feet tall. But he's a brave and good leader of men. Two years earlier, during the Tory ascendancy, he was one of only a few who had the fortitude to resist signing a British loyalty oath. Even I signed one, though only after I was assured that everyone else in the neighborhood had done the same. We elected James Green our captain when the Continental army retook New Jersey and the Tories fled. In the two years since, the Laird family—Robert and my three brothers—have turned out regularly for our bimonthly tours. We rose to the call and marched with the captain and General Forman to Pennsylvania to fight at the Battle of Germantown. Two of our men, Leonard Hoff and Stephen Van Brackle, fell last year battling the Tories, and three more were made prisoners during skirmishes since then.

"I don't know all that's happening today," Captain Green began, "but I do know that the Tories have landed again—and that Captains Smock, Hankinson, Van Cleave, Sweetman and Fleming are all ordered to bring out their men. The Shrewsbury companies of Wainwright and Hampton are ordered to muster, too, though I doubt we'll see many of them today." Hisses rose through the crowd.

James Pearce leaned into my ear: "Today we die to defend thems who won't turn out for their own defense." I nodded gravely at the injustice but whispered back, "But we fight the Tory scoundrels in Shrewsbury so we won't have to fight the scoundrels at our houses."

By one o'clock that afternoon, the captain had recorded who was and wasn't present. We were formed up and began marching the Falls Road for Tinton Falls, minus the disgraceful Albert Schank, who passed out from too much drink ten minutes into the march—our first loss of the day. Across the county, the roads were worse than ever. The Falls Road had ruts and ditches wider than my hips and deep as my shin. Parts were puddled and muddy, and parts were parched earth.

Before the war, the highway overseers hired men each spring to maintain the roads. Our roads were never more than widened dirt paths—we are not fancy people who desire the luxury of cobblestones—but when both men and beast break their legs on the roads, something is seriously wrong. The laborers who used to eagerly work the roads for three pence a day and a canteen of small-beer are now off London Trading with the Tories or, even worse, plundering our farms under the guise of loyalty to the king.

Just a mile into our walk to the Falls, we came upon the state troops withdrawing from the Falls toward Colts Neck. Most were young Freehold men. I recognized half of their faces and knew several by name. Captain Green and Captain Walton of the state troops hailed each other and walked away from the men into a field to exchange information.

Returning to us, Captain Green spoke grimly. "Boys, Captain Walton reports that as many as five hundred redcoats and Tories have landed at Jumping Point. They're returning to the Falls to finish the work they began last April. Captain Walton, with only fifty men, decided he couldn't make a stand against so large a force. So he's pulling back to Huddy's tavern."

Green sighed and looked around. "But the Tory bastards will break up into small parties to sack the farms and private stores of good people. So we'll stay away from any big parties of uniformed Tories, discourage what plundering we can and strike at their smaller parties. Are you with me?" Cheers went up from our ranks, as well as curses and threats on the Tories. I joined in by shouting, "I will bash in a Tory's skull today if given half a chance!"

We continued our march toward the Falls. I was heartened to see Captain Walton give his men leave to follow us. More than a dozen broke ranks and did so. We now numbered over forty. But it was still four more miles to the Falls on a hot, humid day. Although, most of us owned horses, they were too valuable to risk, so we jogged forward for the next hour, stopping just once at a well to drink and refill our canteens.

A mile from the Falls, we smelled smoke. James Pearce whispered to me, "I think the Tories have fired the town." That was confirmed when a man in a storekeeper's apron—I judge a Quaker from his plain dress—came riding up to us. His leg looked broken, and Sam Pearce improvised a splint for it with the handle of shovel and some extra linen we carried for bandages. "The Tories—they're like wild or mad men. They're razing the town. You must help. Please, you must help."

"Steady yourself, Storekeep. We will help you as much as we can." Captain Green attempted to sound reassuring. "But we must know how many of the enemy are at the Falls."

"Maybe fifty. Maybe sixty. Some others are gone to Captain Chadwick's. They have taken Colonels Hendrickson and Wikoff, and others, too. All the principal men in town are taken."

"How many are gone to Chadwick's? I think we should go there."

The storekeeper winced as he adjusted the splint. "Fewer than twenty. The worst of them are still in town, where they're taking everything. They've sacked my store. Captain, I must try to save my store. I must return."

"No, Storekeep, you will help us. I will arrest you and rope your hands if I must. You will guide us to Chadwick's."

The Quaker looked disappointed, but he did as told. He led us south of the Falls, circling a quarter mile to the southeast to avoid being spotted by the main enemy party at the Falls.

We reached Captain Chadwick's too late. The enemy had already been there: it captured the captain, forced his family to flee and fired the house. A black man, slave to Captain Chadwick, I wager, told us that the captain's brother, Jeremiah, and some local militia were pursuing the Tories. They had gone to Jumping Point.

Captain Green discharged the storekeeper with consoling words: "Go to your store and salvage all you can. Tell your friends that the people of Colts Neck and Freehold will be striking up a relief fund for those left suffering, and we will board those left homeless by these atrocious monsters."

Then we jogged another four miles—much of it in the rain—to Jumping Point. But again, we were too late. A terrible fight had occurred between the Shrewsbury militia and the enemy. The Shrewsbury men still at the scene said they had fought bravely despite being outnumbered. But they gave way in hand-to-hand fighting because the Tories had bayonets and they didn't.

During the fight, Jeremiah Chadwick and the Tory commander cursed each other and refused to grant quarter to the other. Chadwick was shot and then run through with a bayonet. The militia had four killed, ten badly wounded and several more with lesser wounds. After a tense standoff in which his life was threatened, a Lieutenant Hendrickson forced the Tories to return several of the wounded. He did this knowing his father (the colonel of the militia regiment) had already been taken away by the departed Tories and lost. I shuddered to think that only a few hours earlier I was lampooning the Shrewsbury men for their lack of dedication.

James Pearce and I collected canteens and brought them to the wounded. We let them drink what remained of our spirits. The poor souls were grateful.

We had jogged twelve miles today but had arrived too late to help our countrymen or smite the Tories. It was time to turn around. It was dark when we walked back through the Falls in low spirits. My head started pounding as the drink wore off. The few stops made for water at local wells did little to replace the water sweated out during the day's marches.

The Falls were a terrible sight. Some of the houses were reduced to smoldering frames and chimneys. Four or five dead bodies had been dragged into a shallow grave and were being buried by two Negroes. It was impossible to tell whether they were militia or Tories. A young militiaman had been blinded when the barrel of his old blunderbuss breached and discharged flaming, scalding powder backward into his eyes. The angry, open scars across the top of his face caused me to turn away. When the wind blew in the wrong direction, the air smelled like burned flesh. It made me nauseous.

Four women, each with small children, came to us and requested food for their children. We offered them what little we were carrying. Captain Green showed them great kindness and promised provisions and shelter for them at Colts Neck. An old woman, Mrs. Williams, came up to us. She told Captain Green that a Tory bandit with a broken leg was at her mill at Eatontown: "He might be made a prisoner, but he's armed. His gang savagely beat a good young man—my boy servant, Billy—before they made off."

Eatontown was only two miles away, so Captain Green asked us if the capture of a Tory might salvage a day of hard marching and late arrivals. Half the men cheered, so we marched again.

It was dark when we approached the house and mill of Mrs. Williams. Captain Green deployed parties of six men each at different points on the road, in the event that the Tory might attempt an escape or to detect other Tory parties returning to carry him off.

Captain Green then looked at the ten of us who remained. "In two groups, we will rush the front and rear doors together." He looked at my cousin Robert, the company's lieutenant, and said, "Laird, you take the Pearce boys, Van Schoick and Richard and rush the rear door. I will go in through the front with my five."

We went round the back of the house as the captain ordered. Robert, ever the protective older cousin, cautioned me, "Richard, you will enter last." But liquor and a desire to prove myself to my older cousin were powerful motivators. I would take the Tory by surprise; he would surrender, or I would kill him.

Before Captain Green gave the signal, I shouldered through the back door. But I stumbled in the threshold as the door's boards splintered between my feet. I fell face first on the floor. James Pearce ran in ahead of me and headed for the back bedroom, where Mrs. Williams said the Tory was lying. Shouts came from the front of the house as the captain's party now entered.

I stood up and ran after Pearce into the back bedroom. I heard the powerful blast of a musket inside the bedroom just as I entered it. James Pearce, my dear old childhood friend, lay on the floor five feet in front of me, wiggling in pain, blood spilling through his hands from his gut. A Tory sat propped up in bed holding a musket, a cloud of gunpowder coming out the muzzle. The putrid smells of saltpeter and a man's guts mixed in the muggy air.

Bleeding from his belly, Pearce looked up at me. "Richard, I will surely die." His face flashed eerie shades of yellow and brown under the flickering candle in the wall sconce.

I gripped my musket and raced forward to the Tory. I fired into him from a few feet away. My shot hit his shoulder, and I watched his upper body jolt backward into a wall. I took the barrel of the gun in my hands and swung it like a club down into his head. The musket vibrated in my hands as the gunstock struck his skull. The Tory tumbled from bed and landed hard on the ground. He cried out, "Ahh…damn you! No more! I am Reap Brindley, and I surrender. I claim the rights of a prisoner of war. You are fair…a Christian man. I am your pris—"

Before he could finish, I hammered him with a second blow of my gunstock. And then I landed a third blow, and then a fourth. My hands hurt, and I was out of breath. I paused and realized that the room was now full with nine men, including Pearce's brother, my cousin Robert and Captain Green. Everyone was watching me.

Captain Green came forward and leaned into my ear: "Richard, you're too far down this road now to turn back. I will take care of the men. Then you'll finish this cursed soul."

Green turned. "Men, leave this house. Form a perimeter at twenty feet. Samuel Pearce, Richard and Robert Laird shall stay with me to tend to the wounded." The other men filed out. Samuel Pearce and Robert lifted James Pearce into the same bed that the Tory had occupied just a minute earlier. James let out a terrible yell. His eyes rolled back into his head, and he passed out. His grief-stricken brother called his name gently and held his hand. James convulsed, and then he convulsed again. The sconce light flickered as he passed to heaven.

By now, the Tory was curled up in a ball, his broken leg trailing unnaturally behind the rest of his body. He sheltered his bleeding head in his hands. "You animal! I am your prisoner. I am your prisoner."

Captain Green handed me the Tory's gun. "The bayonet is a better way to finish this work than clubbing a man." I took the gun and pointed the bayonet at the Tory's head. I had never held a bayonet before and paused to admire the long, triangular blade. I don't know how long I stared at that beautiful blade. Robert waved his hand in front of my face, leaned in and whispered, "This man murdered James Pearce. Avenge our friend."

I gripped the Tory's gun tightly and thrust it downward into his head, but the bayonet deflected off a thick piece of bone and nearly recoiled out of my hands. The Tory screamed in pain and shouted foul words that God forbids me to write. In frustration, I looked to Captain Green. "I want to finish this man. I don't mean him to suffer."

Captain Green patted my shoulder, "Steady, Richard."

I pulled the gun back, regripped it and pushed downward. This time, the bayonet found a crease in the Tory's skull, and the blade slid easily through until it stuck into the floor below. It sounded like melon being split open as a hole opened in the man's head. The Tory was skewered through the skull like a piece of meat. A pungent smell seeped upward.

"Vengeance is terrible work," Captain Green said softly.

Robert came forward and removed the bayonet from the man's head. He used the Tory's shirt to wipe the blade clean. "He's the devil's problem now."

Samuel Pearce muttered quietly, still holding his dead brother's hand.

The men reassembled in the orchard behind the Williams house. They dug two graves. The Tory was dragged out by his heels; his head bounced on each stair. Several of the men, and even the young son of Mrs. Williams, kicked the dead man before he was dumped, face first, into his grave. I was among the four men who carried out James Pearce, wrapped in a bedsheet. We placed a hastily made wooden cross next to the grave of my dear friend—the man who was felled by the musket ball that should have slain me.

We trudged home in the dark and arrived back at Widow West's tavern near midnight. During the three-hour walk, perhaps half the men in our party offered me consoling and encouraging words. The other half wouldn't come near me. I overheard parts of an exchange between the Quaker, Benjamin Jackson, and Captain Green. Jackson said, "My conscience forbids me from turning out with a company that murders a wounded man who has discharged his weapon. He was defenseless." Captain Green matter-of-factly replied, "You know the law, Jackson. You turn out as required or purchase a substitute. We make no concessions to high-and-mighty Quaker moralizing."

At the tavern, Captain Green made a brief statement before dismissing us to our families. "My boys, war can be vicious, and we are fighting a vicious enemy. At some point, each of us will make a decision whether to kill a man who would kill us, kill our wives and kill our children. God will judge us, but while on Earth, let us not judge each other. What happened today, under solemn oath, remains a secret between soldiers, a secret between brothers."

Green took a breath and looked toward Benjamin Jackson. "I will look very sternly on any man who runs his mouth about today's events. I will view any talk of the violations of the rights of Tories as vile disaffection. Those who make talk that threatens to divide us will be punished most severely."

I don't know how late it was when I arrived home. I entered the house quietly. The children had brought lilac into the house, and the hall smelled wonderful. I kissed each of the children—Richard Jr., Margaret, Mary, Elizabeth, Catherine and little William. I said a brief prayer, stripped out of my bloody clothes and slipped into bed next to my wife.

MARY TAYLOR

Libertine

The Revolution was norm wrenching in Monmouth County. Prior to the war, a small clique of squires dominated county leadership positions and steered the courting activities of their children to ensure intermarriage among the "best" families. The war split these families when many of the squires sided with the royal government and went behind British lines. The families who stayed behind suffered the loss of status and property, and many of the squires became estranged from rebellious children.

Mary Taylor was the daughter of George Taylor, the senior colonel of the Monmouth County militia when the war began. In late 1776, George Taylor became a Loyalist and took command of a newly formed Loyalist militia sponsored by the British army. By June 1777, George Taylor was leading Loyalist raids into Monmouth County, and Mary's family became objects of resentment inside the county. Mary's mother, Deborah, tried to hold the family together, but she was rocked by two jarring developments in the spring of 1779. First, pieces of the family estates were confiscated and sold at auction in May. At about the same time, Mary Taylor went off and married a noncommissioned Virginia Continental, John Hagerty, while he was stationed at Tinton Falls. In so doing, Mary chose to step down several rungs on the social ladder and sided against her father.

John and I awoke well rested. Judging by the sun shining brightly through the small window, I guessed it was after 8:00 a.m. There was already great commotion downstairs, but we had slept so soundly that nothing could disturb us.

In the two weeks since John and I married, much had changed. My mother called me "a rebel, a harpy and a buffoon" for marrying John. She said I disgraced the Taylor family name and that my father would beat me when he heard the news of me marrying "a private from Virginia who would never own enough land to properly support a family." She said my marriage would kill my suffering grandfather, Edward. Truth be told, I didn't lose any sleep over the rebuke.

The times have changed. Men like John would have been beaten for courting the daughters of squires before the war. Men like John weren't even allowed to vote or speak at the town meeting. But the old ways are done. John is now the equal of any squire, and I am now a free woman. I can marry by my choice. And John's three years of service in General Washington's army have given him the money to buy a small farm. I don't need the fineries that cloud my mother's vision. I just need the comfort of John's thick arms around me.

I married a beautiful and kind man. In the two weeks since I left Mother's house at Tinton Falls, we have slept like vagrants in the attic of Widow West's tavern near Colts Neck. The widow has always nursed a grudge against my grandfather for some silly ancient reason that I don't pretend to understand, so she lets us stay for free, just to rile the old man. I know that John and I have caused quite a stir among the old disaffected families, even beyond my own, but I've never been happier.

I was already awake and fixing my clothes when John awoke. I heard the rope bed creak noisily, and I turned to see John roll over. "G'morning, Mary."

"Morning, my love," I said as I leaned onto the bed for a good-morning kiss. He grabbed me, and soon we were undressed and under the covers again. I told him, "John, we shouldn't. The tavern's all awake. People will hear us." But our passions swept past my warning. When it was over, we fell back asleep.

We were woken by a pounding on the door. The widow was calling, "John Hagerty! The signal cannon's fired. You're a Jerseyman now. Turn out and defend your state." We were startled into action. In five minutes, John dressed, went downstairs, grabbed his soldier's gear, took a big hunk of cornbread and was out the door.

It would take an hour, perhaps more, for John to jog to the Falls and rejoin Captain Walton's state troops. John had officially enlisted in the state troops a week earlier, but he had requested a two-week furlough from the captain on account of his elopement with me. The captain obliged the request because John's presence at the Falls drove my mother wild, and the captain grew tired of the daily hailstorm of accusations from her. But even with the furlough, John was, of course, expected to turn out on alarm. I worried that his late response to this alarm might get him in some trouble.

An hour later, I was in the great room of the tavern. I had settled at a small table with Phoebe Sutphin, an orphaned girl of thirteen under the care of Widow West. A few days earlier, a teamster employed by the Continental Congress had delivered several hundred musket balls and a box of gunpowder to the tavern for the use of the Virginia Continentals. The teamster didn't know that the Continentals had left the county a few days earlier, and no one was about tell him. For three days, the boxes just sat there in the tavern's great room as men argued over how to divide the arms among the many militia companies. Now that the signal cannons had fired, the three of us hurriedly started rolling cartridges, knowing that Captain Green's men would soon be at the tavern and in need of arms for the day. The errant teamster was God's providence.

Rolling cartridges was simple enough: tear a six-inch square of old newspaper, put the ball near a corner, put a small pool of powder near the middle and roll the paper. With a little practice, I fell into a rhythm—rolling three cartridges a minute. I took some pride in being the fastest cartridge maker of the three women at the table.

Widow West was the slowest. She chattered the whole time. When she tore a square of a Philadelphia newspaper that included a paragraph on the Tory attack on Tinton Falls last April, the widow exclaimed, "Ha! Today, we send this report of Tory barbarities back to the Tory base at Sandy Hook—in the body of a Tory."

It wasn't long before the militiamen started arriving at the tavern, and soon the widow and Robert Laird, whose election as company lieutenant was attributable to his owning a still, were pouring drinks for the men. My parents would have lectured me about the impropriety of being in a tavern with drinking men, but the men showed me no discourtesy. After I finished rolling cartridges, I even briefly played cards with them. They cheered when I downed a cup of Laird's apple spirits, slammed the cup on the table and burped loudly.

I blushed uncomfortably, however, when one of the young militiamen called, "A toast to young Mary Taylor—proof that even the fairest daughter of the haughtiest squire can be bedded down by the commonest rabble in these days of liberty and equality!"

Widow West intervened. "Let's instead toast gentlemanly restraint before an honest young woman who's risked everything for love of country and love of a patriotic young man."

There was a moment of awkward silence. Then Robert Laird shouted, "Huzzah to whatever it was that the widow just said!" All the men laughed and huzzahed.

A few minutes later, Captain Green arrived, and the men were on their way to the Falls to battle the Tories. I briefly wondered if my father or cousin, William, would be out with the Tories today. I knew that Captain Green's men, or John's state troops, might see battle against these Tories today. I winced at the thought of John taking aim at my father and winced again when I pictured cousin William, a fine marksman, taking aim at John. I turned my attention to cleaning up a spilled tankard of small-beer.

By mid-afternoon, I had helped the widow clean up the tavern's great room and was peeling apples for dinner when a boy came into the tavern and pleaded, "There's a wounded man in the cart. Please help."

The widow raced toward the door, and I followed close behind. I saw an unconscious man in the wagon. "Boy, get Dr. Hubbard," I called as I neared.

But the widow was already at the wagon and had assessed the situation. "No, boy, stay here. This man's not wounded. It is Albert Schank, and he had too much to drink earlier today at the tavern. The doctor will just ply him with hot irons and then charge the state for scarring the man's skin. He just needs to sleep this off. Put him to the milkshed; it's cool in there."

About 4:00 p.m., I heard the creaking of wagon wheels coming up the Falls Road and walked out to see a group of men advancing toward the tavern. I recognized two of the men at the front of their column. It was Captain Walton's state troops—John's unit. I giggled with joy, thinking this meant that John was out of harm's way, and ran toward the men.

As I came close, I saw sullen faces, but no blood; no gray gunpowder stains on their clothing. The men hadn't seen combat. I stepped in front of the two men, one whose name I remembered because it was so unusual: Bedford Boltenhouse.

"What is the news from the shore, Bedford? Where's John? I don't see him."

He shrugged. "The Tories landed and must be at the Falls by now. Their party was so large that we could not stand them. The captain is having us fall back to this place." He tipped his hat and started to walk past me.

I grabbed his shirt sleeve. "Bedford, where's John?"

"We have not seen him today, Mary. He didn't make it into camp." He looked at the ground. "But I am sure he's fine."

I lost control and started hitting poor Boltenhouse. "Don't tell me my husband's fine when you don't know. You abandoned him as he was coming out to your camp. I curse you and your lying. And curse all of your cowardice!" I was a whirlwind of flailing arms and kicking legs. I don't know how many times I hit the poor lad, only sixteen years old and no heavier than me.

A large man with a gravelly voice grabbed me from behind, lifted me off the ground and bear-hugged me until my arms hurt in his powerful grip. "Mary Taylor. You will calm yourself. You will calm yourself now, or I will personally bring you to Freehold and lock you in the same cell as your Tory uncle."

I felt cool tears flowing down my hot cheeks. After a few seconds, I calmed down, and the man released me. I turned to face him. It was Captain Walton.

"Now, girl, you go back to the widow's tavern and tell her to prepare food and drink for the men. The widow can draw up a list of provisions provided. I will sign it, and she'll be compensated by the commissary next month."

"Yes, Captain. But where's John?" I asked more calmly.

"Silence, girl. You will do as you're told," he growled.

Ten minutes later, I watched the state troops file into the tavern's great room. As the widow pulled meat pies and cornbread from the hearth, Phoebe Sutphin and I brought out the food to the men. Captain Walton brought out the widow's cask of Madeira wine, her only one, and opened it. His men were soon dipping their cups into the cask and drinking greedily. Apparently, it didn't matter to them that they hadn't requested the widow's permission or that they were spilling as much as they were drinking as a dozen cups and arms bumped against one another. The wooden boards beneath the men turned purple.

The sight sickened me. The cowards had left their post at Tinton Falls and were now feasting in safety. Meanwhile, Patriots like Captain Green's militia and my John were facing the same Tories that these men had enlisted to fight.

If these men weren't going to do their duty, I would do it for them. I snuck out the front door, grabbed two of the muskets leaning against the tavern's front wall and a cartridge sack and started running down the Falls Road.

My father's slave, Ump, had taught me to shoot when I was a girl. These muskets were shorter and heavier than my father's fowler gun, but I would find a stone fence or barn where I could take cover and fire in safety. If I found John, he would help me; so would Captain Green's men.

I had gone less than a mile when I came upon a party of children coming up the road led by a young woman carrying a toddler on her back. I recognized Nellie Wikoff. We had grown up together at the Falls. Nellie was often said to be the most beautiful young woman in Tinton Falls. Her traditional Dutch ways and her father's rising fortune made her the most courted young woman in town.

Her father, Aucke Wikoff, and my father, George Taylor, had been rivals for as long as I can remember. Shortly before the war, the two men came to blows at the annual town meeting. My father, the first colonel of the Monmouth militia at the time, had just selected officers. Even after Wikoff sent his ship to the Caribbean and purchased gunpowder for the men, father would not offer him a commission. He told Wikoff, "Your temperament is too hot for military duty." But Wikoff became the militia's lieutenant colonel a year later when my father revealed himself as a Tory and joined the king's troops. A week after that, Lieutenant Colonel Wikoff searched my house and removed all "military possessions" from it, including a brass-ringed telescope that had been in the family since my great-great-grandfather came over from England.

When Nellie saw me coming, she started crying. "It is awful! The Tories have torched the Falls. They've taken my father and Colonel Hendrickson—and, no doubt, many more of the principal men." She put down her toddler brother, came forward and embraced me like an old friend, sobbing into my chest.

I patted her head a little and offered some words I didn't believe about her father being safe. Growing up, I never liked Nellie, having accepted my father's opinion of the Wikoff family without thinking about it. Now I realized that she'd never said a single unkind thing about me. Even when my romance with John caused most of the people at the Falls to gossip terribly about me, Nellie still offered me a friendly "good day" while others turned their heads.

Looking over Nellie's shoulder, I saw her ten-year-old brother, Garrett, pale and staring blankly. He had a large, raised cut on his head. I went forward and dabbed the wound with the hem of my dress. "What happened to Garrett? He's not well."

"A Tory smacked him with a gunstock when Garrett grabbed his leg and pleaded for Father's release. He's been ghostly ever since—barely saying a word."

I scooped Garrett into my arms and led this sad crew—Nellie, four of her younger siblings and two other children I didn't even know—back to Widow West's. Phoebe Sutphin and I gave them fresh water and the cornbread Widow West kept from Captain Walton's men. The widow and I put Garrett in the widow's own bed and took turns spoon-feeding him a thin porridge. The wound on his head was turning purple. I asked the widow if we should lance it, but the widow waved me away, calling it "part of the body's healing ways." She sang quietly to Garrett.

Nellie came into the room and thanked us for taking such good care of her little brother. Then Nellie changed the subject. "Mary, none of my business, but where were you going with those guns?"

I didn't answer, so the widow filled the silence. "I think Mary Taylor fancied herself some kind of Captain Molly. She was going to run in front of a cannon to save her husband or something equally foolish. Ain't that right, child?" But the widow's tone was much softer than her choice of words.

I blushed and heard myself say, "I just love John so much." I hoped Nellie and the widow understood.

The widow laughed. "Yes, young love is very powerful. But Mary, you're no good to anyone—particularly John—if you get caught up in whatever's going on at the Falls. It won't be a pitched battle like the one fought on the fields near Freehold last year. There'll be small bands of men running around taking shots at each other. Half the time they won't even know if the men they're shooting at are on their side, since they'll all be in day shirts, and the smoke will make it impossible to see. A lone young woman would not change anything—except to a few wild men inclined to do vicious, foul things to a pretty young woman. John needs you here, Mary. I need you here."

Indeed, the widow was right. Over the next four hours, several parties from the Falls came into the tavern. Nearly all the refugees were women and children. By nightfall, the tavern was full with perhaps thirty children of different ages and fifteen women. We also cared for two wounded militiamen who were brought to the tavern in a wagon driven by elderly Altje Van Deripe. We marveled at the old woman for making the two-hour ride from Eatontown at night, despite being almost blind and assumed feebleminded.

I gave my bed to a harelipped mother named Sarah, the wife of a common laborer who had fled her family's cottage when the Tories came through the Falls. Her husband was still out somewhere with the militia. Sarah and her four children were packed tightly together on the bed, and the ropes strained and bowed in the middle. When she found out that she was displacing a squire's daughter, Sarah insisted on vacating the bed, but I would hear nothing of it.

"Your children need a warm place to sleep after such an awful day. You must take my bed," I reassured her.

Near midnight, Captain Green's militia returned. The captain came into the tavern and exchanged some news with the widow. It broke my heart to learn that he had no news to offer about John. Captain Green praised me and the widow: "You have taken good care of those made sick and wretched by today's savagery."

Then he walked into the front yard of the tavern with his men. I listened as he gave them an earnest lecture about soldierly solidarity before dismissing them to their families.

For the militia, the long day ended at midnight. But the widow, Nellie Wikoff, Phoebe Sutphin and I stayed up taking care of crying children and wounded men long beyond that.

Sometime in the wee hours of the night, the tavern finally quieted, and I fell asleep in a chair with my head on a table. I awoke with a start when the front door opened. The great room was dark, and I could see no more than the shadowy silhouette of a person entering the room. Somehow, I immediately knew it was John—something about his quiet walk, about the considerate way he slid the door latch closed behind him when other men would have just slapped the door backward.

I crossed the room, leap-stepping over sleeping children, and jumped into John's waiting arms.

SIP

Black Loyalist

To many African Americans, the American Revolution appeared to be a war fought to preserve slavery. As the 1770s progressed, slaves heard white colonists argue passionately about the inalienable rights of all people. These arguments resonated in African American communities and stoked their militancy. The militancy bridged into war when Virginia's royal governor, Lord Dunmore, declared that slaves who left their rebel owners for British service would be freed at war's end. Word spread to the North, and spurred by additional British offers of freedom, hundreds of New Jersey and New York slaves eventually sought their freedom behind British lines. By the middle years of the war, there was a hodgepodge of official and unofficial black Loyalist groups in and around British-held New York City. Some of these Loyalists participated in raid warfare, particularly those living on Sandy Hook in a semipermanent settlement called Refugeetown.

Sip was a slave from Shrewsbury Township. Based on his subsequent actions, we can assume he was among the militant slaves whose acts—including late night meetings and vandalism—prompted the Shrewsbury militia to confiscate arms and enforce a curfew on all African Americans in the township (even free men). In late 1776, Sip participated in the insurrections that resulted in a brief Loyalist takeover of the county. When Loyalist rule crumbled in January 1777, Sip took a gun and threatened to "put shot amongst" any rebel posse that might come after him. Despite his bravado, Sip was arrested for his role in the Loyalist insurrections and jailed in Philadelphia for four months. In May 1777,

he was returned to his owner in Shrewsbury. After this, he disappears from the
historical record until 1781, when he was arrested in New Jersey with another
African American Loyalist while "in a refugee boat" carrying off goods from
New Jersey farms. So we know that Sip was among the Loyalist irregulars who
participated in raids into New Jersey.

That bastard Gillian woke me in the middle of the night with a kick in the thigh. Groggy and annoyed, I sat up and watched him wake my two mates, Scipio and Jube, in the same rough way. "On your feet, brigands," he said, "a good day's excursion lies ahead. Behave yourselves and you'll have your fill of mutton and coin by tonight."

It was still night, maybe 3:00 a.m., judging by the height of the hazy moon. I put on my hunting shirt and stuffed my blanket into the sack that doubled as my pillow. I tossed it in the shed near the lighthouse. Scipio trailed a few steps behind me and did the same.

Jube, however, did not react to Gillian's call to action. He had been sick with pleurisy since cutting himself in the leg while jumping a fence during our last excursion. The cut had swelled so much that his shin now resembled a ham. He had been running a terrible fever for the last week. He groaned, "Ma…ma" as we left him on the field where we had been sleeping. Jube had seen nothing but bad luck since joining us six months ago. Not everyone was cut out to be a partisan, especially boys like him who had been pampered slaves of godly families.

We left Jube to finish his feverish dreams. There would be no mutton or coin for him today.

Gillian took the path for Horseshoe Bay, where the Loyalist refugees keep their barges. Without saying a word, Scipio and I jogged down the trail to catch up with him. If we weren't at the barges by the time the refugees were ready, they would leave without us. We caught up with Gillian just before the trail through the cedars ended on the bay beach.

I heard several voices near the two closest barges and recognized the Dutch accent of Chrineyonce Van Mater. This was good news. Van Mater was a wealthy man before the war. As a slave owner, he knew the value of Negroes. He was no Quaker idealist who believed in the nobility of the Negro soul, but he understood that black men deserved fair treatment and at least half a white man's share of the day's draw. Refugees like Gillian, oyster-rakers and ferrymen before the war, viewed freedmen like me and Scipio as competitors. At best, we were a necessary evil. I smiled knowing Van Mater would be with us today.

As Scipio and I came closer, we saw other familiar silhouettes by lamplight—there were Donald and Caleb Sweesey, Sylvester Tilton and Barnes Dunnigan. They were Monmouth men like Gillian who joined George Taylor's militia during the Loyalist ascendancy two years ago. When the British quit New Jersey, Taylor's militia fell apart, and the true Loyalists among them fled to Sandy Hook. These men still had family and friends in Monmouth County and used their family ties to find safe landings, go inland, get a few sows and row back to Sandy Hook undetected. Many of these men had been on a dozen excursions already. Sometimes these refugees went north toward Amboy; sometimes they went south into Shrewsbury.

Gillian's friendships along the Middletown shore entitled him to act as our party's co-leader even though we all recognized Van Mater as the better man. In different ways, the years had been hard on all of us, but for squires like Van Mater, I bet it was hard to have to treat men like Gillian as equals. In the same way, I guess, it must have bothered Gillian that he had to work shoulder to shoulder with Negroes. Every white wants to believe he's better than someone else.

Scipio and I fell in with the other men, and we carried out several sacks and ropes for the barges. We knew that the refugees didn't like us handling muskets on our own, so we waited for Gillian to call out, "Boys, help me bring the guns on board." On these words, we went for the guns. I saw Scipio take aim with a handsome English musket and stab at the air with the bayonet. In the early days of the war, the white refugees never let black men handle fine guns like these, but everything was much looser now. Even the officers at the lighthouse now looked the other way when Negroes held guns or wore fancy clothes taken from the rebels. There were too many of us—dozens of black men, and dozens more women and children, now at Sandy Hook. We had proven ourselves equal to whites on excursions. How could they stop us?

After the guns were stowed on the barges, I took several cartridge boxes and wrapped them inside two sacks so the powder would stay dry as we rowed out through the surf. In the early days of the war, we put food on the barges but had long since abandoned that practice—it was easier to get food from the loyal people on the Jersey shore during the excursion.

Ten minutes later, we were out on the water in two barges. The night was still, so there was no point in hoisting our sail. I manned one oar in the first barge, with Dunnigan on the other. After a half hour of rowing, Dunnigan started tiring. He struggled to keep up with me, and the barge veered off to the left, my side. I kept rowing quickly, pretending not to notice that I was embarrassing the white man.

Van Mater steered us back on course. He chided Dunnigan, "Come on, Barnes. Surely a brawny sailor can row harder than a slave." Dunnigan muttered under his breath and attempted to keep up with my strokes. Twice more, I made Van Mater steer the boat back to the left to compensate for my stronger strokes. Then, having made my point, I slowed down a little and let Dunnigan row even with me.

Scipio and Caleb Sweesey rowed the second barge with Gillian at the rudder. They fell in behind us.

We left the cove and were soon out on Raritan Bay. The night was still, and the water was, too. Even so, small drops of water splattered us on each stroke. This was because of the leather straps we wrapped around the oars. The straps kept the oars quiet as they dropped into the water but sprayed water around when the oars came out of the water. The air was misty and thick. Soon, everything in the barge was damp.

Our barges had been built to float hay and livestock down slow, shallow rivers like the Raritan—not flounder about in the open water. Many Loyalists had lost booty or bumbled into capture when their barges overset in the surf. Military men preferred whaleboats, which were faster and easily fitted out with swivel guns. Still, foraging excursions like ours needed barges because they carried livestock—as many as four cows or horses. Whaleboats were too narrow for any animal larger than a sow.

I had personally witnessed a barge carrying six cows on its way back from an excursion. It listed badly, and the men bailed water to keep it from tipping. Scipio and I waded into Horseshoe Bay and helped push it ashore. The men jumped out, waded to shore and kissed the sand. Risks be damned; as long as a healthy bullock continues to fetch £10 at Sandy Hook and £12 at New York, there'll be refugees willing to overload a barge.

An hour more of rowing put us close to the Monmouth shore. I heard Van Mater and Tilton saying that the Jersey Volunteers would be landing at Jumping Point and drawing off the Shrewsbury militia. Gillian's friend Marcus Headon, on the Middletown shore, would make himself a decoy to draw off the Middletown militia dragoons—the only mounted militia of consequence. If Headon's ruse worked, we'd have a quiet morning to gather up goods from the rebels and would likely make Tinton Falls without firing a shot.

Nearing shore, Van Mater signaled with a lamp for Gillian to take the lead. We stopped rowing and let the second barge pass us. Gillian led us into the Conkaskunk Creek.

Although the creek was narrow and shallow, the flat-bottomed barge settled in perfectly. Dunnigan and I stopped rowing and used our long oars as poles. Quiet was now all-important. All conversation stopped.

Just a hundred yards into the creek, Van Mater pointed over my shoulder. Two of the men on Gillian's barge splashed into the water and pushed their barge toward a dim light on the shore. The first hints of sunlight made it a little easier to see around us. It was a perfect landing spot for two barges: tree-lined on both sides, with a firm bank—ideal for driving off livestock. Gillian was a mean bastard, but he had done well in getting us this landing.

Dunnigan and I dropped into the water and started pushing our barge. The creek water chilled my body, and my feet sank ankle-deep in muck. I shivered as Dunnigan and I shoved the barge onto the bank. Gillian picked up the lantern and pointed to a collection of leafy cedar branches off to the side of the bank. We covered up the barges as best we could with them. If the day went according to plan, Van Mater would return in them tonight with half our party, while the other half would push through the Falls to Jumping Point, where two more barges would be waiting by afternoon.

Walking up the trail, I caught up with Scipio and gave him a friendly shove from behind. He stumbled forward into Caleb Sweezey's back. He harshly whispered, "Mind your steps" and shoved Scipio backward. Scipio and I giggled; so did a few of the men.

Gillian came down the path and punched Scipio in the chest. "Quiet, nigger! The rebels could be on this shore." His whisper barely contained his anger.

I wanted to pummel Gillian for this and his many other bully moments. My hands balled into fists, but I held back. I hated Gillian. Back at Sandy Hook, Tye and some of the other black men were talking with the British about getting our own boats and guns. Then black men would be able to launch our own excursions. But until that day came, we needed Gillian. My fists unclenched.

We put our gear into two wagons left for us by Headon and were off.

The first house we came to belonged to the old Quaker Robert Hartshorne. He and Van Mater spoke like old friends even though Hartshorne's brother was the paymaster for the rebel militia. Hartshorne's daughters brought us smoked fish and bread, which we ate as we continued toward the Falls. The sun was up now.

Crossing Hartshorne's land, we came onto the Falls road. We climbed out of the wagons. Van Mater and another Dutchman drove the wagons but stayed back. The seven of us—Gillian, the two Sweeseys, Tilton, Dunningan, Scipio and me—went ahead on foot.

We passed through narrow woods and came into a clearing. A boy—maybe fourteen—was plowing a small field near us. There were two other men on the opposite end of the field. Gillian jogged ahead and hailed them. "We are the king's men. Come forward slowly. We mean you no harm."

The two men on the far end of the field bolted into the woods. Scipio and Tilton took up the chase, but the rebels had too big a lead. Scipio and Tilton soon returned. The boy brought us to his house—a handsome two-story home with whitewashed cedar shingles, scalloped at the bottom. I saw a large barn and pen full of pigs. I smelled the smoke of a busy kitchen as we came near. I knew there would be a fine meal at this house and perhaps more.

Van Mater spoke in Dutch with a woman named Hulse, who ran the house. She had a stern face. I heard her call us "Tories" and knew she was not a good woman. Van Mater directed Dunnigan and Scipio to search the house for arms. The rest of the men, including me, turned to the kitchen where Tilton was slicing a loaf of bread on the table. He then put the knife— with a fine bone handle dyed jade green—in his pocket. "A knife for a brave man in the king's service won't be missed on this prosperous farm."

Dunnigan and Scipio returned to the kitchen and offered a mocking tip of a cap to the rebel woman. Dunnigan pulled a stew pot out of the hearth with a hook. Soon we were dunking our hunks of bread in the stew pot. The mutton was moist and fresh and mixed with turnips and wild onions—the best meal I had tasted in months. After our bread was finished, I dunked my hand into the pot and scooped up the remaining stew pieces with my three middle fingers. I saw disgust in the eyes of the old rebel woman. So I smiled and stuck my hand into the pot again just to see her sour expression. Van Mater wrote her a receipt for what we brought out of the house, plus the three cows I roped.

In the yard, Scipio showed me a handsome pewter fork he put into the interior pocket of his overshirt. He handed me a ½ inch cylinder of sugar with a broad smile.

As we exited the house, Gillian called, "Missus, my Negroes have empty hands. Help us fill their sacks. Fetch us two fowl, and we'll be gone from your fine farm." We waited, but no one came out.

Gillian nodded, and I went into the chicken pen. After a brief chase, I cornered a fine white hen. I turned to see that Scipio hadn't followed me to the chicken coup but went into the pigpen and was carrying a well-fed piglet. We laughed as I stuffed the chicken in my sack and he dropped the fat piglet in his.

We jogged down the road to Van Mater. He met us with the two wagons. We dropped our sacks into the wagon and each picked up a little bag stuffed with cartridges. The easy part of the day was over.

It was time to meet the Jersey Volunteers and take the Falls.

It took an hour to travel the four miles to the clearing where we'd meet the volunteers. To my surprise, there was another party of refugees waiting for us. Van Mater recognized the leader. He called out, "Huzzah to the great rascal, William Clark!"

The two leaders embraced. But the men in Clark's party—ten in total—looked at us harshly. A large young man with boils on his face and huge fists pointed toward me and Scipio, whispered something to his mates and they all laughed. Van Mater looked crossly at the laughing men and called, "The black men are fine partisans. Mind your manners, you pirates!"

The big man moved toward Van Mater. I readied myself for a brawl, but Clark intervened. "Elisha Grooms! Sit your big arse down now. You will save your fightin' for the rebels." The big man backed away.

Twenty minutes later, the Jersey Volunteers arrived. You could see their red and green coats at a distance. These men were "Provincials," Americans who joined the British army, mostly in 1776 and 1777. But for all their months of soldier drilling and fancy coats, these men were no better than me and Scipio. They lived in tents and froze in the winter, just like black men. A few were gaunt, and others carried the awful scars of camp fever on their hands and faces, just like black men. They marched in formation and wore nice coats, but what did that really matter?

The two officers came in wagons. There was Moody, a tall man with a Scottish accent, and a Lieutenant Okerson, whom I recognized. He had been a merchant at Shrewsbury before the war. I saw many familiar faces among their party.

Gillian, Van Mater and Clark went off with Okerson and Moody into a stand of trees, leaving the men a few minutes to wash their hands and feet in the stream. The water was cool and fresh. I let it run across the crusty and caked scabs on my feet and ankles.

Okerson returned to the river and spoke to us. "All right, you brigands. We divide into five groups: Van Mater will take half of his men and head back to his barges with the rebel seizures so far today. The volunteers will split between me, Ensign Moody and Mr. Clark. We will head for the Falls and surprise the rebel militia officers. The refugees will be put under the charge of Mr. Gillian. They will visit Captain Chadwick, south of the village."

On news of being put under Gillian, Scipio flashed me a look of concern. I understood but gave him a shrug and a little smile, not wanting to reinforce his unease. But I was just as worried as Scipio. My fears calmed a little when we saw Lieutenant Okerson's brother, a sergeant, join us.

After hiking a mile through marshes, our crew came within sight of Captain Chadwick's. The large white house backed up to the swamp but was flanked by well-improved farmland and orchards on both sides. Like so many of the big farmhouses in the county, it had started as a one-room home and had since had a two-story, multiroom addition built onto it. The original house now sat attached to the main house as a kitchen. We paused before the clearing.

Gillian spoke. "Load your weapons. But don't fire. We must have surprise. Captain Chadwick is valuable to us alive; he's barely worth the clothes on his back if he's dead." He looked at young Okerson. "Do you have any last advice before we go into your childhood home?"

Okerson blushed and looked away. "I don't know, Gillian. There's not much to say. That bastard, Chadwick, chased my father from town and took possession of the house two years later."

"Talk about the house. Where do you think Chadwick sleeps? Where will he keep the guns? Are there any older boys who might cause us trouble?"

"He will probably sleep in my father's bedroom toward the back of the house, ground level. Chadwick has two grown sons who should be with their uncle Jeremiah and the militia today. Two others are old enough to fire a gun—Gabriel, about fifteen, and David, about thirteen. They should be in the fields by now. They could be a quarter mile off with the way the farm stretches south from here. I reckon if we're quiet, they won't even know we've come to, eh, visit their father. But there are a bunch of young ones who'll be about the farm and house this time of day. There's also a smaller house not too far off where Jeremiah Chadwick lives with a whore."

The men laughed a little.

Gillian cut them off. "Jeremiah is the captain's younger brother and as vicious a persecutor of Loyalists as his brother. But boys, don't get distracted. We are here for the captain. Then we take war materials: guns, wagons, livestock. If they cooperate, that's it. If they don't cooperate, you listen to me, and I will decide on appropriate retaliation. We stay close together, except you Negro boys, Sip and Scipio. You cross to the front of the house and stay outside. Watch the road for any approaches. Shoot anyone who flees the house."

Scipio blurted, "Will we get a share of today's draw if we're watching the road?"

Gillian turned and spat at Scipio's feet. "Nigger, this is war. and you're a soldier for the king. If you don't get your own draw, that's too bad. But if you do your job and mind your manners, you'll get some of the draw."

Gillian shoved Scipio backward. The men laughed a little. "Quiet down, boys. Don't mind me with talking hard with the Negroes. It's all they understand."

Scipio and I did as we were told. When Gillian rushed the house, we crossed in front and stood sentinel between the house and the road. Over the next twenty minutes, as best I can tell, Gillian's brave white Loyalists grabbed up the sleeping captain and tied him around a tree in the yard, escorted the women and children from the house, took every portable item of value and loaded a wagon with their plunder. The party got careless, and the family slave scurried away with a horse and a small wagon. Claiming this was an act of defiance, Gillian set fire to the house. From the road, I watched the rebel mother and a young daughter cry as their house burned to the ground. Young Okerson stood off to the side; he wept also.

Hearing some scattered shots in the distance, I knew that the other parties had struck the Falls, and any militia on hand would be busy harassing the volunteers. The roads were clear; no one would be threatening us. My mind wandered a little.

By now, I had participated in many excursions. I had fired barns and outbuildings, taken a dozen men prisoner and even beat an old man for saying he would "take no direction from any nigger, even one with a musket." I never felt any remorse for these actions—the rebels had done worse to me. But watching the young daughter of the rebel captain weep affected me. I've never admitted this to anyone, but I had to wipe away a tear as I watched the girl cry.

It took another hour to fully gather up the Chadwick family's possessions. Gillian had fired the house too quickly, preventing resourceful partisans like me and Scipio from picking through the bedrooms. The fire made the livestock uneasy, and they were hard to yoke. The biggest horse jumped its stable when the refugees came close. I watched it trot down the Falls Road without a rider—a good day's draw for two men was lost when that big rump escaped.

The heavily loaded wagon was pulled by a single overburdened horse—the lone remaining horse from Chadwick's barn. This slowed our withdrawal toward Jumping Point. Behind the wagon trailed the dozen pigs and sheep of Captain Chadwick, who was bound and gagged at the back of the convoy. The poor horse was so overburdened that we had to push the wagon through muddy spots on the road. Judging by the sun, it must have been about four o'clock by the time we reached the shore. As prearranged, there were two barges waiting for us there. But the tide was withdrawing, so the barges sat fifty feet from shore, separated by a steady drumbeat of two-foot waves crashing on the sand.

The next two hours were miserable. The weather grew darker, and the distant thunder made the animals jumpy all over again. Our wagon overset in the surf as we tried to push it out to the barges, scattering everything. So we waded into waist-high water fetching barrels of pitch, small casks of spirits, bedding and the captain's desk as they drifted out to sea. We recovered most everything but lost precious time. Then Gillian singled out Scipio and me to steer the crazed-with-fear livestock through the water and haul them up on the barges. A pig lunged upward in the surf and smashed into my chin. I bled all over it as we wrestled the remaining ten feet to the barge and then tied a rope around its thrashing, panicked body so the bargemen could pull it in.

Only a few of the livestock had been loaded when one of the volunteers standing sentry on the beach shouted, "Rebels coming down the road!" Gillian started barking orders that were drowned out by the noise of the ocean. I left a lamb to fend for itself in waist-deep water and ran back toward our guns.

The rebels came down the road and pitched themselves amongst clusters of bushes and high grass. They got off a volley, and one of their shots caught Caleb Sweesey with a ball in the arm.

I saw Gillian and Dunnigan pulling the wagon from the water, hoping to get it onto the beach for cover. I ran to help them, and together we got it in front of our supplies and tipped it over. Scipio, Tilton and two of Clark's men found good cover one hundred feet away behind a felled tree trunk. We fired back.

Between fires, Ensign Moody and the rebel commander shouted insults at each other. The rebel commander called us barbarians, scoundrels, banditti and bastards. From his tongue, I knew he was certainly no better.

He shouted, "I am Jeremiah Chadwick. You have taken my brother, run off his family and burned his house. I shall avenge him.

I will kill each of you, dismember your bodies and cast your limbs into the surf. Do not call for quarter; it shall not be granted."

Gillian shouted back, "And the only mercy you will receive from me is that I will kill you quickly instead of running you through and leaving you to watch your blood turn this beach red. I will not ask for quarter, and you will not either, for by damn, I will kill you with my bare hands after you surrender."

The firing kept up for another half hour. With both parties well hidden, I don't think that anyone was hit. But the firing on the rebel side became less frequent. Gillian whispered to me, "Run across to the log where Tilton and the others are. Tell them that the rebels are running low on musket balls. We will charge on my word."

I looked Gillian in the eye, "Running in the open is madness. They'll kill me."

Gillian punched me in the chest, "Do it now. I am your commander." Then he softened. "Do this for me and prove that you deserve a full share of today's draw. Prove to me that a black man can be as brave as a white man. They're low on cartridges and will not fire. I know it."

I counted to five and then ran across the beach to the log, kicking up sand as I dove headfirst behind the tree trunk with Tilton, Scipio and five other Loyalists. One or two muskets discharged at me during the run, but Gillian was right, the rebels were running low—my run proved it. I told the refugees that on Gillian's word, we would charge with our bayonets. We saw a line of Jersey Volunteers advancing up the beach to reinforce Moody's line.

Then Gillian called, "Forward now, my boys. Skewer the rebels!" We stood and ran toward the berm that sheltered the enemy's closest line.

Lieutenant Chadwick came up over the berm, waving his sword wildly. He shouted to his men, but most did not go forward with him. As he shouted, Ensign Moody took aim from twenty feet and fired a ball into him. Chadwick dropped to his knees holding his belly. The refugees came up, and Elisha Grooms ran a bayonet through Chadwick's back. Our party ran past, and a dozen Loyalists tumbled over the berm and engaged the rebels. A few shots fired at close range felled two rebels, and our bayonets lanced four others.

One rebel fought us like the devil, swinging his musket like a club, catching Grooms in the head and sending him headfirst into the sand. He swung again and knocked Scipio onto all fours with a heavy blow to the back.

I jumped on the rebel's back, and we wrestled in the sand. He was stronger than a bull and flipped himself on top of me. He punched me in the jaw, and I bit my tongue. Blood poured into my mouth. He raised his fist to hit me again. Then Scipio's bayonet came through his back and out the front of his chest. He fell forward on top of me, his warm blood soaking my body. He coughed and gurgled as I pushed the dying brute off me.

A rebel yelled, "Fall back!" and a dozen of them scrambled into the woods. Gillian tackled one of the fleeing men and stabbed him with a knife through the back of his neck. The battle was over. I was wet; I looked up to see that it was raining. How long had this been going on?

We had killed eight of them, including Lieutenant Chadwick, and wounded another eight. Despite Moody's battlefield curse to grant no quarter, we accepted the surrenders of these wounded wretches and did what we could to dress their wounds. Scipio and I searched the dead bodies for valuables and found some coins, a nicely tanned leather belt, two canteens with spirits and shoes for my feet.

As I stuffed the coins in my pocket, Gillian looked at me sternly. I prepared to hand him the goods that I had pulled off the corpses. He laughed and said, "Just hand me the coin and take the rebel weapons to the barge. Keep the rest. You and Scipio will guard the prisoners while we drive the rest of the stock onboard."

I kept a gun on the wounded men. Scipio tied the prisoners together by the feet and then moored the rope to the overturned wagon. The salt breeze was now blowing in; the sun reappeared, and my feet were enjoying the feeling of leather shoes. I drank down a canteen of spirits, even though it stung terribly in my bloody mouth. I watched the other men as they wrestled the livestock out to the barge. The men toiled as Scipio and I finally enjoyed some easy time. The Jersey Volunteers pushed off in their barges.

A half hour later, at dusk, our work was nearly done. All that was left was carrying the wounded onto the second barge. Scipio and I motioned the men toward the water. Then two shots rang out from the woods, and I saw them splash in the water. Scipio and I dove for the ground and began crawling toward the tree trunk. We made it. I fired off into the woods but couldn't see the enemy.

Three more shots came toward us, and the tree trunk jiggled on each impact. Gillian jumped off the barge with two guns and waded to shore. The day's draw was fully loaded; he could have gone off. He fired a shot into the woods as he crashed in the sand behind Scipio and me.

A thin young man came out of the woods with a white flag. "I am offering terms of a truce. Terms of a truce," he repeated.

Gillian stood up and pointed his gun straight at the man. "Hold your hands high or I will shoot you dead right now!"

The man stopped. "There are thirty men with guns in the woods. You cannot make it to your boat without being shot. Free the prisoners, and we let you get off. Those are the terms."

"If you fire on us, we will smite you again. I can kill you right now!" Gillian shouted.

"You cannot get off this shore without my men having a fine shot at you. You will die in the surf, and more militia will arrive if you delay. Consider that. Give us our wounded, and we will let you go."

The rebel was right. His party might not have the bayonets or courage to take us on the beach, but we had no escape either. The long, slow wade to the barge would be our death.

Gillian looked at Scipio. "How many of the prisoners are fine enough to come with us to the barge and then swim back from the boat?"

"Two, maybe three," he said.

"Good. Tie those men to you and set the others free on my order."

Gillian stood up again, dropped his gun and walked toward the thin man.

"I will give you some of the prisoners now. But I will keep three with me. They will come with me and my men to the barge. When

91

we get onboard, all but one will be released. We keep the last man as security and will run him through if you fire onto the barges. He will be at Sandy Hook and available for ransom if you want him. Those are my terms. There is no counter offer."

The rebel hesitated and then offered his hand. Gillian shook it. Gillian waved his hand, and Scipio and I cut the ropes from the feet of five of the wounded men. Gillian walked backward toward the wagon, eyeing the woods. It was twilight, and we could not see the enemy. My heart raced.

Gillian grabbed one of the remaining wounded and put his knife against the boy's throat. He then walked the boy backward into the water. Scipio and I tied ourselves to the other prisoners, grabbed them close and followed Gillian.

The rebel guns stayed silent. We jumped onto the barge. Scipio and I released our prisoners; Gillian kept his. The released men waded to shore as the bargemen pushed us off into deeper water and raised a square lateen sail.

A brisk evening breeze carried us quickly from shore.

JAMES HULSE

Reluctant Revolutionary

There were many types of Revolutionaries. Some paid taxes and served in the militia but sought to minimize the impact of the war on their lives. However, local events—particularly vindictive Loyalist raids—pushed many reluctant Revolutionaries toward more affirmatively serving the cause. In the parts of Monmouth County close to the British/Loyalist base at Sandy Hook, many families supported the Revolution, but they did so with reluctance. They understood that their homes and livestock were more likely to be targeted when their families' men took up arms.

The Hulses were a large but modest family spread across the northern half of Monmouth County. Most of the family weathered the war by doing only what was required of them. John Hulse, the apparent patriarch, owned a 150-acre farm in Middletown and laid low throughout the war. Only one of his sons, Matthias, volunteered for military service. Matthias enlisted in the Continental army for six months, during which time he narrowly escaped capture, became very ill and was discharged early. A few months later, he was captured while serving in the militia and, while in prison, nearly died from illness. Another son, Timothy, served in the militia. A third young man in the family, James, is listed as a "Single Man" in the 1784 tax rolls and did not serve in the militia. His poverty and lack of military service suggest that James was living as a dependent, possibly an orphan.

It was still dark outside when I woke. I looked out the small window in the loft. I whispered, "Not a star in the sky." I remembered a story my mother told me as a boy about starless skies bringing bad luck. I could feel that it was already warm, even at 5:00 a.m. It would hit ninety degrees today. Were it not for last April's raid, the wealthy families at the Falls would have used the warm weather as an opportunity to quit their fields early, get drunk and race their horses into the night, disturbing the sleep of the pious people who lived along the Falls Road.

I inched out of the loft, not wanting to stir my two younger sisters, who were still sleeping soundly. A few narrow beams of light cut unevenly up the ladder from the candles lit below in the kitchen. In the dark, I changed my nightshirt for my day shirt, pulled up my work trousers and stockings and climbed down on a ladder no wider than my head.

On my way down, I hopped over the second-to-last rung, with its splintered board. I had torn my stocking on this board twice. Uncle John had told me to "quit my indolence" and fix it, but it was easier to avoid the offensive board. My sisters had learned to step over it as well.

"G'morning," I mumbled to Sukey, the lone slave of Uncle John. Sukey gave a polite smile and continued tending the large pot from which I would soon eat breakfast. Because it was a warm morning, I took the chamber pot and went through the kitchen into the milkshed to relieve myself. I did this as a small favor to Sukey. She could leave the waste unattended in the milkshed until after breakfast.

By 5:30 a.m., most of the house was awake. Uncle John; my oldest cousins, Matthias and Timothy; and I were eating breakfast. The girls were now awake and awaiting their turn at the table. Matthias always took a little longer than the other men—he coughed terribly each morning, a lingering effect of the jail fever he caught while a prisoner in New York. Between his wheezes, he complained that breakfast (a porridge of different grains, water, wild onions and small pieces of dried ham) wasn't nourishing. I knew that Matthias should be thanking God that we had any food in these hard times, but I held my tongue. He had suffered terribly these last three years and felt entitled to complain.

Matthias was right about breakfast. It had become less satisfying in the six months since my sisters and I started living with Uncle John's family. It went unstated, but we all knew that our arrival was the reason the family could no longer purchase extra meat and fish. But even impulsive Matthias knew not to complain about the arrival of his orphaned cousins. Uncle John would have surely whipped him. Being a war hero earned him no special treatment from Uncle John.

Matthias, instead, turned his discontent upon Sukey and her son, Jube, who had run off. He grumbled, "When we could loan out Jube, we could always buy salted fish to eat with breakfast. And Sukey's not working as hard as she did when Jube lived with us." Four months earlier, Jube had run off on General Clinton's proclamation of freedom for slaves who would serve the British. It caused great commotion in the household. There were accusations that Sukey aided the treachery. Matthias threatened to beat Sukey when she wouldn't denounce her boy for leaving. I secretly worried that my sister's and my arrival in the house pushed Jube to run off. We took the loft where he and Sukey used to sleep. After that, they had to sleep on the kitchen floor through the long, cold winter.

Whatever the reason, the loss of a strong-backed slave was a big blow to the family and proof again that, no matter how he tried, Uncle John couldn't keep his family unaffected by this awful war. Uncle John, as he always did when the war came up, deflected Matthias's harsh words back to workday topics, saying, "God is minding Jube and Sukey, you need to mind the fields. I see that the north field is not yet sewn with winter rye." Like many of his generation, Uncle John had spent the last twenty years learning to suppress his Dutch accent, but it was still evident when he was irritated. Listening to him over pronounce the "u" sounds in Jube and Sukey, I knew he was plenty angry at his son for picking on Sukey.

It happened about 8:00 a.m. I was plowing and seeding the north field with Timothy when a small party of armed Tories came jogging

down the Falls Road toward Tinton Falls. Amid the grunts of the
ox and the sucking sound of the muddy soil turning over, I hadn't
heard or seen them until Timothy shouted, "Tories!" I looked up
to see him running for the woods. Their guns were trained on me
before I could do the same.

A tall man in a green coat drove up in a wagon and called,
"Come forward slowly. We mean you no harm." I knew the coat
meant he belonged to one of the old Tory units. I inched toward
the men.

He introduced himself as "Lieutenant Chrineyonce Van Mater
of the King's Loyal Militia" and told me that his men would do
no harm as long as my family showed them "hospitality befitting
the king's soldiers." As I led the men toward the house, we said
nothing to one another. But I turned red when I heard one of
the men joke, "Even if we come up empty today, we will return
with full bellies and warm dreams of the lovely daughters of the
Hulse family."

As we approached the house, I saw my sister, Margaret, and my
cousin, Elizabeth, bolt for the woods. Two of the Tories started after
them, but the men reluctantly returned when Van Mater shouted,
"They're only frightened children, let them go!"

At the house, Aunt Huldah, my nine-year-old sister Altje and
Sukey brought the men as much food as we had. Van Mater praised
the women for their "loyalty and hospitality" and promised that no
harm would be done to the family.

As the men ate greedily, I stood at the edge of the kitchen and took
measure of this party of king's men. There were nine in all. Two
were Negroes. I didn't like seeing Negroes mistreated, but it angered
me to see black men armed and lounging in my uncle's kitchen,
being served by my aunt and sister. The Negroes looked about the
same age as Jube, and I wondered if Jube was also out picarooning
under arms, imposing himself on peaceful, godly families who had
never wronged him.

The Negroes and most of the king's men lacked shoes. Besides
Van Mater, they all wore dirty shirts and trousers. Only Van Mater
had any military attire at all—a green soldiers' coat. Were it not
for the guns, they could be easily mistaken for laborers or sailors. I

recognized one man to be Barnes Dunnigan, only three years older than me. Before the war, my father had hired him as a teamster, and I remembered Dunnigan and my father arguing over wages. Seeing Dunnigan reminded me of my father's tragic death six months ago at the hands of Tory bandits.

The men were not careful and forgot about me when Aunt Huldah brought them fresh bread and honeycomb. I could have fled, jumped on my uncle's horse and alerted Captain Chadwick at the Falls in twenty minutes. But Uncle John had given strict instructions about how to act if the Tories came. He said, "Wars makes corpses, not heroes. A hasty exit to alert the militia will endanger the family and the house. Stay home and look after the women and livestock. If the Tories want anything valuable, appeal to their officer for mercy, but if the officer is a hard man, let them take what they want."

The war had been difficult for Uncle John. He nearly lost his oldest son when Matthias went off to serve without his father's consent. Then, Uncle John lost his older brother, my father. Uncle John used these hardships to underscore that the only course for his family was to be like the Quakers and "be a friend to everyone in the world." I had my doubts about Uncle John's pacifism but obeyed his order. So I stayed put outside the kitchen.

As the men finished eating, Dunnigan and the Negroes searched the house under the pretense that we might be hiding arms. Van Mater and Aunt Huldah spoke quietly in the corner of the kitchen in Dutch. Though it was the language of my grandparents, I barely knew more than a dozen phrases. I was only able to make out a few stray words from their conversation, but I could tell from Van Mater's moderate tone and Aunt Huldah's posture that he was reassuring her.

The Tories found no arms but brought a few shirts, shoes and trousers into the kitchen. They put on the new clothes as we watched. Van Mater took inventory of these items, wrote them down on a small slip of paper and gave it to Aunt Huldah. The inventory of items included the clothing and three cows, now roped by one of the Negroes and visible from the kitchen window.

Van Mater briefly argued with one of the men about whether to take the two horses in the barn that a Negro had taken out. Van

Mater cut off the man's protest with a wave of the hand. "We must eat, and we must have clothing, but we don't need the horses of these inoffensive people." He gave Aunt Huldah the piece of paper and said it authorized her to be reimbursed for the lost property. Then the party was gone.

When the men exited, we searched the house to see if anything else was taken. We discovered that the Tories had also taken my uncle's silver snuffbox and shoe buckles (the only silver items we owned) and several small kitchen items, including our green-handled forks and the remainder of the family's sugar cone, which Aunt Huldah was saving for Uncle John's birthday in two weeks. They also carried off a piglet and hen in a sack. None of these items were on Van Mater's inventory. Although the Tories were still in the front yard, we did not protest. Aunt Huldah, Altje and even Sukey wept as the cows were driven off.

After the Tories disappeared down the road, I called for Timothy. He came out of the woods. He told us that Uncle John and Matthias had run into the woods when they saw the Tories. Uncle John told his sons to watch the house from a safe distance. Then, ignoring his own standing counsel, Uncle John went to the Falls to alert the militia. After Uncle John left, Matthias ran down the road to alert our neighbors and get a gun. Matthias had not returned, but we reassured ourselves that he was safe with Uncle John or a neighbor.

Timothy and I ran back to the house. Aunt Huldah reminded everyone never to provoke armed parties. "God will protect us better than any musket." Then she looked at me. "James, you must ride toward the Falls to find and retrieve your uncle John and Matthias." Timothy protested and said he would go with me, but Aunt Huldah reasoned, "James is the better horse rider, and we need a man here." When Timothy argued, Aunt Huldah snapped, "Timothy, you *will* stay or you will be damned." It was the only time I ever heard Aunt Huldah swear. He stayed.

We searched the house, but the family's musket was gone, so I took our best knife and tied it across my back. I saddled our fastest horse, a black mare named Princess Charlotte, and was off.

I had not gone more than a mile toward the Falls when I saw a party of state troopers advancing up the road away from the Falls. A harried-looking sergeant at the front of the party called out, "Boy, take your horse off the road. Let my men pass."

I asked a sergeant why he was leaving. He didn't reply. I approached John Van Hice, a resident of the Falls whose enlistment into the state troops nearly caused a riot when his father tried to force his release. (Mr. Van Hice claimed his son was made drunk by the recruiter and then "deluded" with lies about the service.) Despite knowing Van Hice my entire life, he kept his stare forward and didn't acknowledge me. Five times I called, "Johnny, tell me what's happening?"

So I turned to a wart-covered woman who trailed the troops and asked her for any news. She replied, "It's like April again. The Tories have landed at Jumping Point, and the men are falling back to Colts Neck." She cautioned me to turn around. "Fair son, turn back from the Falls."

I had to find Uncle John and Matthias and get them out of harm's way. I stopped at the houses of our nearest neighbors, the Vuncks and the Vorhees, but both were abandoned. The lack of livestock in their yards was a bad sign. I steadied myself with the knowledge that I had a fast horse and could change course quickly. The woods were thick, and I knew them well. As I rode forward, I called out the names of the wildflowers along the roadside, attempting to ignore my racing heart and trembling hands.

A half mile away from the Falls, I smelled smoke in the air and saw Nellie Wikoff, the daughter of Lieutenant Colonel Aucke Wikoff, the wealthiest man in all of Shrewsbury Township. I fancied Nellie but recognized that she was destined to be married to a man from a wealthier family. Nellie was leading five children away from the Falls. When she saw me, she rushed forward. "James, it is the most terrible thing I have seen. Worse than April's attack!" She brushed away tears. "The Tories have put torch to my father's house and the

THE RAZING OF TINTON FALLS

public magazine in Colonel Hendrickson's barn. They're burning other buildings in the village." She paused. "James, they have taken my father and Colonel Hendrickson."

I asked her about Uncle John and Matthias. She looked at me with her sweet blue eyes and said, "I have not seen them. But it's all smoke and confusion at the Falls. I could've walked right past them and not known."

"Is the militia resisting?"

"Some Middletown men are taking popping shots at the Tories from the village edges."

I told Nellie to seek shelter at Uncle John's house. "Thank you, James, for your kindness, but I am going to Huddy's tavern in Colts Neck where the state troops might offer a family like mine greater protection than your family can provide. On my arrival, I will pray for your family's protection."

She then grabbed one of the youngsters by the hand and started walking again. The two youngest children were crying; her ten-year-old brother was carrying a toddler piggyback despite an ugly wound to his head, and Nellie had a baby in her arms. I wondered why she was leading this party of Wikoff children without assistance from Mrs. Wikoff or any of the family's slaves. I wondered why the family had split up but dared not ask.

I passed two other parties of women and children as I came upon the clearing in the woods that looked down on the Falls. I heard some firing in the distance. I could now see the village of Tinton Falls—twenty or so buildings. They were speckled with red and orange flames and plumes of black smoke. I counted seven buildings burning.

To my right, I saw a group of perhaps a dozen militiamen firing and reloading. I recognized a few of them. They were Captain Smock's men, and they had come all the way from Middletown. I thanked God for their bravery. A party of perhaps thirty Jersey Volunteers, bright in their red and green coats, advanced deliberately toward the militia. The Middletown men fired another volley and then fled into the woods.

One of the Tories fell. The blood from a wound in his thigh soaked through his breeches. A corporal shouted at me, "Come forward, boy! I need your horse to assist this wounded man." I turned and galloped away as he cursed me.

Not finding Uncle John or Matthias, I raced toward home past the Vunck farm. I saw a party of perhaps ten Tory robbers, half of them on horses carrying the brands of Middletown families. I shivered at the thought that they must have already come past my house. A mounted Tory with a Dutch accent was out in front of them. He called, "Halt, young rebel!"

I steered Princess Charlotte into the woods. I heard shouts and looked back to see three mounted men pursuing me. Though tired, Princess Charlotte was still fast, and I steered her down a little deer path into a bog. The bog would slow me down but might prove impassable to encumbered Tories on unfamiliar horses. I heard one Tory curse the mud as he plunged into it. They broke off the chase.

When I was sure the men had stopped pursuing, I dismounted and walked Princess Charlotte through the woods. I fed her some wild onions and rested briefly at an old hunter's cabin. I remembered the cabin. Perhaps ten years earlier, I had trailed my father through the same stretch of woods on a deer hunt. I wished my father and mother were still alive, but I thanked God for sending me to Uncle John and Aunt Huldah, who treated me like their own son.

I circled two miles south through the woods and came out on the Falls Road again near the field where I had first spotted the Tories—near where the terror had started this morning. I mounted Princess Charlotte again and galloped for home. It was near dusk, and I realized that I had not eaten anything since breakfast, twelve hours earlier. I felt hungry and hoped Sukey had prepared some meat for dinner. Coming near, I prayed Uncle John and Matthias were safe at home.

As the woods cleared, I smelled smoke and saw flames coming through the roof of the barn. The acrid stink of burning manure and marl, fertilizers piled near the barn, made me cough and wheeze. Uncle John's house was standing, but the windows were broken out. I could see all kinds of farm and home items strewn about the yard.

I rode forward and wept with Aunt Huldah and the children for the next two hours. After nightfall, Uncle John returned home. He told us about reaching the Falls and alerting Captain

Walton of the state troops. Captain Walton quickly concluded, "The Falls cannot be defended against so powerful an enemy." His men began their withdrawal within fifteen minutes as Uncle John watched slack-jawed.

Uncle John fell in with the arriving Middletown militia and skirmished with the Tories, but the militiamen were driven off when the Tories charged. He showed me a hole in his cartridge pouch made by an enemy musket ball that passed through it.

Near midnight, Matthias returned. As we spoke and wept together, the events that caused the Tories to fire the barn and plunder the house came into focus. Matthias had alerted our neighbors of the coming of the Tories and was given a musket at the Vorhees house. He returned home to find a second party of Tories at the house; this group was not moderated by a gentleman like Van Mater. Matthias explained, "It made me furious to hear the Tories speaking harshly to your Aunt Huldah for saying that there was no food because another Tory party had eaten it all. As a Tory went into the yard and started counting our hogs, I fired and hit the man in the back." Matthias then fled into the woods as three men came forward and fired at him.

In retaliation, the Tories fired the barn and sacked the house. Their leader turned a blind eye. Uncle John told us, "By firing, Matthias had cast our family as 'rebels,' and the officer would not restrain the men from exacting Tory justice on the family of a rebel who attacked one of their party." But there was no anger in Uncle John's voice. He paused and inhaled. "We should thank God for protecting our bodies and our souls. Everything else will be replaced."

Long into the night, Uncle John, Aunt Huldah, Matthias, Timothy and I talked about what to do next. Uncle John would send the smaller children to live with his surviving brother, William, near Freehold. The adults, Sukey and me would stay at the house to rebuild. It pained me to hear this, but Princess Charlotte would be sold for cut boards, glass and nails. We would sleep on the bare kitchen floor together until Uncle John and Timothy could repair the beds or improvise some bunks. Matthias would join the state troops; the bounty would allow us to buy an old milk cow and wagon. On my sixteenth birthday, in September, I would also join the state troops. The recruitment bounty would let the family buy essential clothing in time for the cold weather.

We quietly prayed together and finally went to sleep. Tomorrow would be a better day.

SARAH CHADWICK

Child of a Revolutionary Leader

Battles are fought between soldiers, but wars impact the entire population. The Loyalist raiding parties that came over from Sandy Hook and New York to attack New Jersey did so primarily to plunder and settle old scores with the most strident Revolutionaries. These raids inevitably impacted families, including children, who were often in the way. When the raiding parties arrived, children frequently came in contact with the raiders and suffered in the aftermath.

Sarah Chadwick was a daughter of Captain Thomas Chadwick, the most active of Shrewsbury Township's eight militia captains. When the Loyalists arrived to destroy Tinton Falls on June 10, 1779, they targeted the Chadwick family. The Chadwicks were likely a target because Thomas Chadwick was a militia officer but also because, a few weeks earlier, the Chadwicks had moved into a house confiscated from a Loyalist family. The Loyalists broke into the Chadwicks' new house and took Thomas Chadwick from bed. Sarah Chadwick likely looked on as this event transpired.

I was supposed to be helping Mommy pile the dishes after breakfast. But mostly, I was playing with my favorite doll—the beautiful porcelain one Daddy brought me all the way from Philadelphia a year ago. The top part of the Dutch door in the kitchen was open to let in the morning air. The climbing roses were blooming outside and smelled very good. Even inside the kitchen, they smelled good. Mommy said the roses were her favorite thing about our new house. Everyone in the family liked something different about our big, new house. For me, it was the painting of London—with its fine buildings—above the parlor's fireplace. I would put my doll in front of the painting and imagine her walking down London's busy streets.

David and Gabriel, my fourteen- and twelve-year-old brothers, left the house to begin the day at the farm. They would be gone until dinner. Father was still in bed, and my oldest brothers—Jacob and Samuel, sixteen and seventeen—were staying with Uncle Jeremiah and the militia. So my younger brothers, just a few years older than me, had to work all day in the fields with our slave, Joe.

It all happened very fast. I heard steps on our stoop and a shout, "Stand still, everyone! You are rebels answerable to the king again. My men have guns at all exits of this house." Two large men in fancy red and green coats stuck their guns into the kitchen and pointed them at Mother. I screamed and ran behind her long brown dress.

Mother patted my hair. "Careful child, screaming won't help. Settle down now."

The first man reached over the Dutch door and unlatched it. They entered the kitchen. We heard a crashing sound at the back door, and a big man came into the kitchen from the other side of the room. Their guns had huge knives at the end. They were pointed at Mother.

"You will take us to Thomas Chadwick. He is under arrest," the big man said to Mother.

Mother stood. "Aye, but please don't touch the children. They play no part in this war." The big man nodded.

Mother looked at me. "Sarah, baby, you stay here. Mommy will be back very soon. Stand still, and the men won't hurt you."

I don't know how long I stood there, but I was still as any person can be. After what seemed like an hour, I saw the men come downstairs with Father, who was still in his nightshirt. Father looked sick; he had gone to the tavern with Uncle Jeremiah last night to celebrate Uncle's return home from sea. Father always woke up early—except on the nights he went out with Uncle Jeremiah. Now, Father's face was whiter than his shirt. The only color anywhere on his body was in his eyes—pink and watery. The men walked him through the kitchen. Father called to me, "Courage, my Sarah! Remember, Daddy loves his children more than anything." The men hurried him outside.

A wagon pulled forward. It was carrying Colonel Hendrickson, Lieutenant Colonel Wikoff, Captain McKnight and Major Van Brunt. They put Father on the wagon and drove off as a dozen Tory soldiers jogged alongside.

The big man came back into the kitchen.

"Missus Chadwick, ma'am, you must leave the house. Take your daughter and go outside now. I am sorry, ma'am, but I have my orders." For all this man's size and weapons, there was nothing scary about him anymore. He looked small and sad.

Mother took my hand, and we went into the yard.

From the yard, I looked back into the kitchen through the Dutch door. I could see the men bent over the hearth but could not see what they were doing. They walked into the hallway and front parlor and bent down in both rooms. Then they ran out of the house. Within seconds, I saw smoke coming out the open windows on the ground floor—and then ugly orange flames.

Mother cried, "You horrible animals! We have done you no wrong. I helped you carry off my husband, and still you do this." Then she yelled even louder, "AND my baby, Eliza, is sleeping upstairs! My baby, damn you!"

Mother ran into the house. One of the Tories followed her. From the window, I watched the Tory take off his coat and swat down the flames on the staircase so Mother could pass upstairs. A minute later, Mother came running back down the stairs with little Eliza in her arms. She ran outside, the hem of her dress on fire. The Tory ran behind mother, swatting at the fire on her dress with his coat. Another Tory doused Mother's legs with a bucket of water. There were shouts and grunts from all three as they put out the fire on Mother's legs. But Eliza's loud crying covered their words.

Mother looked at the Tory who had risked his life. "You're a brave young man. But I will never thank you. You serve kidnappers and murderers—and now you have ruined my family's life. Leave us alone. Let me gather my children and fowl in peace. We cannot save the house. Your evil work is done."

For a while, I watched the fire and cried while Mother wet the singed ends of her dress. Then, Mother started looking around.

She sent me off to the barn to saddle the horse. But I had just reached the barn when I heard shots coming from the little bridge over Eaton's Creek. A militia party had come up. They fired at the line of red and green men between my house and town. One of the Tories at my house fell. The other Tories ran off, but only for a few minutes. Soon, I heard shouts of "Form up! Form up!" The Tories, now maybe forty of them, were coming back in a neat line under a big flag. When I heard a military drum, I knew it was bad for us. The Tory soldiers came forward in a line that stretched into the yard of my house.

I ran back to Mother. We looked both ways. There were now lines of men with guns in front and behind us. Baby Eliza was still crying.

Mother put herself on a knee. "Sarah, we cannot stay here. We must run for the bridge and get behind the militia. Run for the bridge. NOW!" And we did. A round of guns fired behind us. A musket ball kicked up dirt in front of me.

As we came close to the bridge, Mother called out, "It is Elizabeth Chadwick. Don't fire! Hold your fire!" Shouts of "Hold yer fire!" went up and down the line of militia.

We raced across the bridge, ran through the line of militia and stopped at the foot of a big tree twenty feet behind the men. Mother pulled up her dress to the knee—the skin on back of her legs was dark red and shiny with a watery covering. Looking at it made me cry. Little Eliza kept crying in Mother's arms.

"Sarah, darling, be a good girl and go the stream. Wet the bottom of your dress. Mommy's skin is a little bit sore. She needs to put something cold and wet on it. Go upstream, sweetie. And, no matter what, stay away from the men—even if it means leaving Mommy alone for a little while. Do you understand?"

I nodded.

"That's my big girl. Now, stop crying. Go now."

I ran back toward the stream. The Tories were moving closer to the militia, and now the two lines were separated by only the narrow stream and maybe thirty feet of my father's new farm. A few of the Tories shouted down their line, "Charge bayonets!" They fired and came forward, splashing into the stream. The militia fired one more time and then ran off. The Tories chased them, running past me and then running past Mother.

When the militia scattered into the woods, the Tories cheered and threw their hats into the air.

I went back to Mother. Gabriel and David had found us and were with her now.

I sat next to Mother and let her dab my dress on her ugly burns. She squeezed Gabe's hand on each dab. His eyes bugged out real big on each of her squeezes, but he never budged or peeped. David held Eliza. She kept crying.

For the next hour, we watched our new house burn to the ground. Mother nursed little Eliza in plain sight of the Tories. No one said a word.

The Tories pulled out of town about 2:00 p.m. After they left, people came out of their hiding places. Some went to help the wounded. Most shoveled dirt onto the flames.

Joe, our slave, came across the bridge with a wagon. It was half filled with pots, plates and other things from our kitchen. "The fire didn't take up in the kitchen right away, so I was able to save some things." He reached back into the wagon and raised up my doll. I ran across the little clearing and hugged him.

Joe and Gabriel helped Mother into the wagon. Her legs were now purple, and she cursed under her breath as they moved her. I jumped in the back of wagon, sitting on top of our Dutch oven.

Joe drove us to Uncle Jeremiah's house—a two-room cabin that the Tories ignored because it was small and off the road. Uncle Jeremiah had no family, just a girl servant named Silence. She helped us into the house. We made Mother as comfortable as we could—putting her in the rope bed in Uncle Jeremiah's little bedroom. We propped up her feet and dripped cool water on her legs.

At sunset, we settled in for a strange dinner. Silence didn't have enough food for us, just some cornbread and berries. But Joe went back to our farm and returned with a huge block of cheese from our milkshed that Mother was hoping to sell at Mr. White's store. It had not fully hardened yet, and white liquid dripped from it. But we were hungry, and the food filled our bellies. No one complained.

After dinner, Silence and Joe switched the room from kitchen to bedroom. They pulled out two large blankets from a chest and set them on the wood floor. Since Uncle Jeremiah's cabin didn't have a loft and he didn't have a barn either, Joe had to sleep outside. He's a good slave, and we love him, but everyone knows he cannot sleep in the same room as my ailing mother or a little girl like me.

Silence laid down across the top side of the blankets and invited us to use her body as a pillow. She's a good servant to Uncle Jeremiah and very kind to us children. I don't know why Father calls her a word I am not allowed to say. I laid down between my brothers and put my head on her little belly. Soon, she was snoring, and my brothers joked about Uncle Jeremiah needing to change her name.

I listened to my brothers as they talked about Father. Gabriel said that Father would be put on a prison ship. I was happy to hear this. "Daddy loves sailing. He might enjoy his time as a prisoner." Gabe said, "Dumb girl, the prison ships are rotten hulks that sit in New York Harbor. They are awful floating jails—men die every day from jail fever and want of decent food and water."

But my brothers were even more worried about Jacob, Samuel and Uncle Jeremiah. Gabriel lowered his voice, "With every minute they're gone, it is more likely that they was taken, hurt or even killed."

David said, "Don't talk like that—you'll scare little Sarah."

"You don't scare me. Jacob and Samuel are good with a gun and run fast. No Tory could catch them. And Uncle Jeremiah is the bravest man we know—you even said that yourself, Gabe."

After a while, my brothers fell asleep. I made myself stay awake, waiting for the door to open and for my brothers and Uncle Jeremiah to walk in. They are safe. I know it.

The door never opened. Sometime that night, I fell asleep.

THOMAS OKERSON

Loyalist Officer

Many Americans were Loyalists—people who risked their lives and property to oppose American independence. Recent immigrants from Great Britain and wealthy families with ties to the British government were among those most likely to become Loyalists. Many of these Loyalists supported the early protests against British policies, but as the colonies moved toward independence, their sympathies switched. A few days after the Declaration of Independence was passed by the Continental Congress, sixty Monmouth County Loyalists marched off to join the British, and Loyalist associations formed across the county. Over the next year, more than five hundred Monmouthers enlisted in the New Jersey Volunteers, a Loyalist corps within the British army. As the war dragged on, these Loyalists emerged as key participants in the raid warfare around Monmouth County.

Thomas Okerson was the son of Samuel Okerson, a Loyalist whose estate was confiscated by the Revolutionary government. Just two weeks after the signing of the Declaration of Independence, Thomas Okerson was arrested for speaking out against the new government. In the following months, Okerson distinguished himself as an active Loyalist and was rewarded with a lieutenant's commission in the New Jersey Volunteers. In December 1776, he led a Loyalist posse to arrest a local Revolutionary leader. His apparent zeal led his superiors to caution him, "[You] are on no account to touch his life." Okerson fled Monmouth County when the British quit New Jersey in early 1777, but he was captured later that year by the Continental army. Okerson was forced out of his command in April

*1778 and retired at half pay when the New Jersey Volunteers consolidated
battalions. However, he remained active in the local war, serving as a guide in
the April 1778 raid that razed the saltworks at Manasquan and the first raid
against Tinton Falls in April 1779 (six weeks before the June 10 raid). Later in
the war, he was recommissioned as an officer in the King's American Rangers—
another Loyalist corps. He and his younger brother, John, were captured during
an incursion into New Jersey in November 1782. John was convicted of murder
and hanged, but there is no record of Thomas even being tried. As an officer in the
king's troops, Thomas was likely exchanged for an American officer of the same
rank in British custody.*

My little brother, John, is only seventeen. Most days he's kept
busy as a waiter to the officers at the Sandy Hook Lighthouse.
But today he'd be needed in his other role—as a guide to a party of
refugees and New Jersey Volunteers on excursion to Tinton Falls.

John awakened me as he does most mornings, rapping gently on the
door of the bedroom of the lighthouse keeper's cottage. "G'morning,
sirs, time to rise if it be your pleasure." Ever the dutiful one in the
family, I am proud how well John has taken to military hierarchy. So
many Loyalists who were comfortable before the war—every man
fancying himself deserving of a colonel's commission—chafe at the
close quarters, the lack of provisions and the loss of privilege that come
with military life. But John has never once complained.

The sun was not up yet. But from the window, I could see a small
red glow over the ocean horizon. From my bed, I stretched my leg.
Two months ago, I pulled a calf muscle when I slipped on a lingering
patch of ice, and it's still stiff and painful each morning. I had lunged
after two Negroes who had come into the lighthouse keeper's yard to
steal a chicken. The black men have proven themselves fine pirates
when turned loose on the rebels, but they're only trouble when idle.
My calf is proof of that. I flexed it gently and then placed my foot
in a sheet and gently pulled my toes upward. The muscle burned as
I stretched it.

Sam Leonard, Joe Throckmorton and I currently share the
bedroom in the keeper's cottage—which serves as quarters for the
junior officers residing on the Hook. Last fall, several good officers,
including me, were taken out of active service when the battalions

were consolidated. I was a prisoner of war when it happened. They "retired" me at half pay. But I remain zealous, and there remains a great need for men like me in raising provisions for the active soldiers. Twice already this spring, despite the insult of being retired, I've led men into Monmouth. I would do so again today.

The cottage has two rope beds. One has frayed ropes, creating a hole in the middle. We cut cards each night to see who will sleep on the sagging bed and who will have to sleep on the hardwood bunk brought in from the enlisted men's barracks. Sleeping on a hard bunk is beneath the dignity of any officer, but we are all making sacrifices. Sam, Joe and I have known one another for years and would not be so unmanly as to complain on drawing the low card. When Joe was bedded down by a fever last week, he was excused from cutting cards altogether and given the good bed. Such is the honor and brotherhood among the active and inactive officers of the New Jersey Volunteers.

I limped across the room, stirred the coals in the fireplace and tossed a small cedar log into the fire. The red embers sprung to life, and a small flame quickly lit the log's rough edge. The room now glowed orange. After a short spell with the chamber pot, I poured some water into a small pot that hung from a hook and pushed the hook over the fire. I felt along my night table and found the desired object; I dropped my curling iron into the water. I dressed: white shirt, white trousers and red and green coat. Retired or not, I still had my officers' coat. Sam still pined for the green coat and brown hunter's frock that we wore in 1777, but even he admitted that adding red to the uniform was a good step toward putting us on better footing with the British officers.

The water had now heated the curling iron just right. I clasped its cooler edges and wrapped the iron around my hair, twisting it upward from the shoulders. Some officers, especially Sam, saw no value in fussing over appearance on excursion days. Sam even said it was dangerous, tipping off the rebels that we were officers. We had heard stories about the rebels targeting Burgoyne's officers before the disaster at Saratoga. But I disagree. The men respect officers who look like they should be officers. And besides, the Jersey shore is filled with lovely young ladies just waiting to be impressed by dashing young gentlemen in the king's service.

I kid Sam that we have a responsibility to look our best. "It is not for vanity but for the common weal. We do it for those comely lasses who, through no fault of their own, must daily cast eyes upon Captain Shoe-Black and Lieutenant Cordwainer of their pettifog militia. It is our responsibility to show them what a real military gentleman looks like."

Even though it was too dark to see much in the mirror, I could tell my curl was perfect by running my hand from my ears backward. I topped my head with my cocked hat and poured the hot water into the cup John left for me. The water moistened the ground tea leaves, and it warmed my spirit to sip the results. Sam and Joe would stay back today to command the men at the lighthouse. I was off on an excursion to Tinton Falls with fifty-six Jersey Volunteers—half from my old company and half North Jersey men under Ensign Moody. We'd be joined by whatever collection of irregulars wished to picaroon on our flanks.

The horizon was just turning orange as I neared our barges. Moody, well known for his attention to detail, was already at the water's edge. He was barking at the men about double-counting cartridges, forty rounds for each, and ensuring that each barge was loaded with thirty sacks. Moody's attention was perhaps overcautious, but no harm in that. He had also divided the fifty-six volunteers among the barges. I watched the men begin to board without so much as acknowledging me. I tried not to take offense that the presumptuous Ensign Moody, my junior in rank, had seen fit to divide up men formerly under my command and spread them among his volunteers. Perhaps I would have words with the ensign about this at the end of today's excursion.

Moody saw me and tipped his hat. "Thank you for joining us today, Lieutenant." I did not appreciate the insult, particularly in front of the men, but I would be the bigger man. "The pleasure is mine, Ensign. I am impressed by your industry. You are indeed a Scotsman."

He half bowed to me and pointed past Captain Heyden's gunboat to the far barge, the largest in our three-boat flotilla. At least he remembered that the higher-ranking officer is entitled command of the bigger vessel. Several of my men saluted as I neared the barge, but some, tussling with stores and readying the boat, did not. I looked sternly at John Worthly, my former sergeant. "Sergeant, tell the men that an officer is coming aboard."

Worthly stood straight and called, "Lieutenant coming aboard!" All of my men immediately dropped their tasks to stand at attention. Moody's men rounded themselves to attention, too, but with noticeably less spirit. Given the example being set by their officer, this didn't surprise me.

With four long poles, we pushed off and hoisted sail. I kept our flotilla a quarter mile from shore where the current was strongest but brought us near the shore at the bottom of the Hook to avoid the sandbar. Moody may fancy himself the Duke of Marlborough or Alexander the Great, but we both know that my knowledge of the shoreline is central to our excursion's success. Six weeks ago, I played a key role as a guide to Colonel Hyde and his regiment of British regulars when we forced the Continentals to flee Tinton Falls. No less than the colonel himself had called my knowledge of the local waters and roads "indispensable" to the success of that excursion. The winds were mild, but the currents were favorable, and we made good time, reaching our landing spot at Jumping Point at dawn.

We disembarked, Moody's small barge first and my large barge last; the captain's gunboat would cover our descent and protect our barges through the day. Moody, behaving more like a sergeant than an officer, reformed the men into his ad hoc units as they disembarked from the barges. When the men had been formed, I came ashore. "Fine work, Ensign. I shall now lead the men to the Falls. Please have a corporal's guard stand sentry on the beach. You shall bring up the rear." John and a few of my men snickered at the insult.

It was only three miles to the meeting place, and we arrived there by 7:00 a.m. I knew that as long as we stayed off the Falls Road and traveled via Hartshorne's abandoned estate, the slow-witted rebels would never be alarmed. Indeed, all was quiet as we signaled our arrival to the irregulars and fell in with perhaps forty of them a quarter mile above the Falls.

The irregulars called themselves refugees, but that broadly used term might confuse them with gentlemen like me or George Taylor, formerly the colonel of the Monmouth militia and now a Loyalist. These men clearly were a different species of refugee—the rebels called them cowboys, and I called them picaroons. Whatever the name, they were little more than pirates who claimed loyalty to the king to gain access to vessels and the protection of the king's troops. To look at these ruffians was to know they were unreliable allies, hardly better than drunken Indians. They made no attempt to look like proper men—stubble-filled faces, rags for clothing and carrion smells that might alert the rebel militia if the wind were blowing in the wrong direction. Yet all the senior officers, right up through General Skinner, insisted that we show these men every courtesy. And truth be told, the goods these men brought in were important to keeping the soldiers fed and clothed during the increasingly long stretches between British provision convoys.

In any event, Moody and I had little choice but to grant the leaders of these men an informal war council as they were nearly as numerous as we. They would be needed on our flanks today if we were to overawe the rebel militia.

Moody and I went off to a clearing with their three leaders. I was pleased to see that among them was Chrineyonce Van Mater. I did not know him well but knew that his was a good Dutch family. His uncle, Daniel, was among the first Loyalists to leave Monmouth County in July 1776. The Van Maters bought land on Jamaica Bay on Long Island and had been more successful than most Loyalists in reestablishing their yeomen ways in New York. In the warm months, however, Van Mater continued to picaroon up and down Raritan Bay with his more rough-hewn partner, William Clark, the vulgar-mouthed son of an honorable and loyal physician. The other leader of the picaroons was William Gillian, an oyster-shucker by trade who had used the war to parlay his only asset—a gambler's love of risk—into a small fortune by plundering the countryside with his band of sailors and Negroes. I detested having to treat a man like Gillian as a peer during excursions, but such was the standing order.

After receiving salutes from Van Mater, Clark and Gillian, I spoke. "Gentlemen [I flattered them], we arrive at this place unnoticed by the rebel guard. If we are as smart as we are brave, we shall have surprise with us on our arrival at the Falls. Before we transact any business raising provisions for the king's troops and Loyalists, our first order is to capture the most infamous Loyalist persecutors in town: rebel officers Hendrickson, Wikoff, Van Brunt, McKnight and Chadwick." I showed them the map I had drawn of our approach to the village and the houses of our five targets—four in town, and the fifth, Chadwick's home, just south of town.

I proceeded to assign a senior member of our party to each of the houses and described how each party would approach through the ravine that passed west of town. Our parties would storm each house on the signal of my pistol. If the rebel officer and family cooperated, there was to be no retaliation on private property. "But if the rebels resist, Ensign Moody and I understand that the fire that burns inside aggrieved Loyalists might flame up. And we will not discipline the men who harbor so many great and terrible grievances—as long as they show good judgment to confine themselves to rebel property." I then proceeded to name a dozen good families in the neighborhood that would be off limits to the men.

To his credit, Moody nodded dutifully through my presentation of the day's plan of action. He seemed to understand that with my knowledge of the neighborhood I should lead the day. The overeager junior officer was properly obedient.

Gillian raised concerns for the safety of the goods the picaroons had already taken from farm families on their way to our meeting spot. I rolled my eyes and chided him, "Your zeal for sheep and household trinkets cannot trump military necessity, Mr. Gillian. If your sheep wander off while we are taking the town, that is of no concern to the king. But understanding that it would distress your men and make them less inclined to fight today, Mr. Van Mater shall take a corporal's guard of your least capable men and carry away your booty."

"You shall come to Tinton Falls with me, Mr. Gillian. Take your fine Negro soldiers and seize my father's house—now in the possession of the ruffian Chadwick. If the family resists, you shall fire the house. We will show no sentimentality for the house just because it is the rightful property of my father. He will be well compensated by the Commissary for Refugees if necessary. You will have John Okerson, my brother, with you to assist in maintaining fidelity to the orders of the day."

A half hour later, our parties positioned themselves at the edge of town. A few farm boys were seen heading to the fields, and I saw the Quaker merchant Britton White head out of town down the shore road in a wagon. My party—myself, Sergeant Worthly and ten of my old company—would take the home of the town's most vile rebel, Aucke Wikoff. (I cannot bring myself to call him by the rank of his rebel commission.)

Before the war began, Wikoff had seized the private property of any family with connections to the government—including mine. He insulted my father near daily, and when my father challenged Wikoff to a duel, Wikoff and a gang took my father's dueling pistols. He pried out the brass inlay and sold them. Wikoff said he was justified because my father refused to sign the treasonous Continental Association.

Then, Wikoff stopped paying the debts he owed to my father or anyone else he termed a Tory. By renouncing his debts and flooding the town with the rebel government's money, Wikoff went from being the town's biggest debtor to creditor in a fortnight. A month ago, Wikoff and his clique had gone too far—moving Captain Chadwick into my father's house. My father, made frail by age and rebel cruelties, wept when I told him that Chadwick—a man of low talents and lower character—now occupied his house. Today, I would avenge my father.

I fired the signal shot in the air, and my party rushed Wikoff's house. Worthly pushed his thick body through the back door and, after a few shouts from inside, signaled to me that the house was secured. I entered. Wikoff was sitting at his breakfast table with his wife, their young children and his lovely seventeen-year-old daughter, Nellie. I stepped heavily, letting my heels echo on the wooden floorboards in the now silent house.

I tipped my hat to Nellie, whom I had fancied greatly before the war. Her full bosoms were more alluring than ever. "Men, be on your best behavior. There are ladies in this house who should not be tarred by the hateful disposition of their kin." I smiled at Nellie Wikoff. I thought about how I might still court her after the war, when order is restored.

"Aucke Wikoff. For the crimes of high treason, taking up arms against the king's troops, sedition, larceny and, no doubt, many other offenses, I hereby arrest you in the name of King George III. You shall come peacefully with me, Lieutenant Thomas Okerson."

Wikoff glared at me. "You will hang, Okerson. And when you do, I will grease the rope and tie the knot."

I nodded, and two of the privates moved close to him with their bayonets lowered toward his chest. "Curse you all, damn Tories," he muttered. But he stood up and meekly went to the wagon as my prisoner. Brazen words and cowardly conduct—the way of the rebels.

I called to Worthly, "Sergeant, take the wagon and gather up Hendrickson, Van Brunt, McKnight and Chadwick. If they carry themselves like officers and stay in the wagon, show them proper respect. If there are any liberties taken, you are ordered to bind their hands, tie them together and blindfold them."

The other parties secured their rebel potentates with the same ease. The first objective of the day, to seize the worst traitors of the town, was done. I paused to thank God. Then I looked down the road to see Gillian's party fire my father's house. Since John was with that party, I knew the act was justified, but I still choked up.

The next two hours went well. The rebel militia briefly showed up on the fringe of the village and fired a few ineffectual volleys, wounding one of the men. But when Moody called "Form up!" and the soldiers formed a line, the rebels backed away. When the men charged, the rebels displayed their only useful combat skill—the ability to withdraw quickly. They headed off into the woods and swamps south of town. Moody and a few men mounted the villagers' horses and briefly pursued them, but to no avail. We received no further challenge that morning, except scattering another militia party who approached from Middletown. They fired on our picket and were driven off by two well-leveled volleys.

The noncommissioned officers then formed up the men and, consistent with General Skinner's orders, proceeded to bring in military materials from the rebels, including guns, wagons and horses.

I sent Worthly with a wagon to gather up grains from John Williams's mill and sent John to the Blue Ball tavern to carry off its spirits.

As the men impressed these and other goods, they issued certificates for everything they seized. Using Wikoff's house as my headquarters, I signed a dozen receipts from Wikoff's desk. The rebel families, under a flag of truce, would go to Sandy Hook and receive just compensation from the commissary officer upon presentation of the receipt.

Many families thanked the Loyalists for taking their ill-fed stock. The gold coins and New York money the country people would receive at Sandy Hook could buy twice as many head on their return into Jersey. Most of these families brought eggs and wool with them to the Hook and traded them for more British coins, proving that most of the country people were only cowed or deluded into supporting the rebellion. They were all too happy to hold honest trade and communication with the king's troops.

If a rebel family sought to prevent the king's troops from completing their assigned business, General Skinner also gave us permission to make the frontier safer for the king's troops by forcing those rebel families inland. Yes, under the eye of an officer, my men did put torch to Colonel Hendrickson's barn because it held the rebels' arms and then put torches to the homes of Wikoff and Chadwick. In these latter two cases, the families took actions that endangered the king's troops, and firing the house was the appropriate countermeasure. However, even in these cases, my men only fired the homes after the people were removed. Contrary to rebel propaganda, true Loyalists do not plunder and certainly never murder.

The picaroons—Gillian and his band of sailors and Negroes—were different. John, Worthly and the other noncommissioned officers reported numerous disorders committed by the irregulars, including taking cider and wine from private homes, removing the tools from the smith shop and robbing the local store—a place known to be owned by the inoffensive Quakers Britton and Benjamin White. I spent two hours hearing the petitions of different aggrieved villagers, a few of which engendered my sympathy and action. Four times, I dispatched noncommissioned officers to curb the worst excesses of my ungovernable allies, but alas, I know that we did not correct every disorder.

By two o'clock in the afternoon, we had completed the day's objectives. The rebel leaders of Tinton Falls were taken and secured, the rebel militia was smited and scattered and a well-regulated impressment of military materials and livestock had netted us an impressive haul. I inventoried our seven wagons: three loaded with cartridges and powder, two more loaded with food and drink and one loaded with the day's most peculiar haul—three dozen four-pound cannonballs. More importantly, we had rounded up nearly one hundred head of livestock. The costs were light. One of my former men, Job Chamberlain, was shot in the thigh. His wound was well dressed, and he reclined in the seventh wagon on a bed of straw befitting an officer. The ease of the day and the size of the haul evoked my generosity.

Moody organized the men into a line of march, and I appointed John "chief drover." He was sent out of town ahead of us for our barges at Jumping Point, with twenty men, the wagons and the livestock. I called to Gillian, "Remove your vagabonds from this village." But he protested that his men needed more time "to press more war materials."

I groaned but let the ruffians stay behind. I didn't need forty unsatisfied picaroons whispering foul rumors the entire march back. I marched out of town immediately after the drover's train with Worthly's men. We would provide the force necessary to dispatch any threat should the rebels ride down on the livestock. Moody's platoon would bring up the rear; I was happy to let the Scotsman have the honor of fending off any new attacks from the militia, knowing their ranks would swell and they would make another descent on us by day's end.

I was uneasy about leaving Gillian behind. He would certainly bring down a reign of lawless mischief on the village, but I could not endanger the mission by protecting rebel savages from loyal savages.

Although Jumping Point was just a few miles away, it took us two hours to complete the march. John's men did their best to drive the livestock quickly, but the narrow road and the mass of skittish animals conspired against us. So did the weather, which grew dark and windy as we reached the shore, further spooking the animals. The cows were particularly difficult, often sitting down as we neared the shore, forcing the men to whack their butts with gunstocks. We were so bogged down that Gillian's irregulars caught up with us at Hartshorne's plantation, a mile before Jumping Point.

I heard some popping shots from behind; the rebel militia had reformed and was now engaging Moody's men in some running fire. Like moths drawn to a lantern, more militia would soon be falling in on our flanks.

Upon reaching the shore, I had my men and Gillian's irregulars take to the surf with the livestock. The horses went easily, but the cows and goats put up a terrible fuss. Moody's men set up a line at the top of the beach and exchanged shot with the militia, who secreted themselves in the bushes nearby. It was now overcast, and I heard thunder in between the gunfire and braying animals.

After perhaps fifteen minutes of overseeing this commotion, with only a few of the livestock loaded, Moody sent a man to me. "Lieutenant Okerson, sir, Ensign Moody requests that your men reinforce him on the beach." I looked up the beach to see Moody's men pulling back and reforming behind a waist-high sand berm. Two Loyalists, made prominent by their red and green coats on the light-colored sand, lay slain. Another man from Moody's platoon crawled on all fours toward his comrades.

I looked at the private, "Go back to your officer, private, and tell him that Okerson's men are coming." As the private ran back to his platoon, I could not help whispering, "So the haughty Scotsman who treated me as an encumbrance now needs me to save him."

"Worthly, John, form up your men. We are going up the beach to drive away the rebels. Gillian, get your brigands out of the water and form up on the lower shore. I need your men to maintain a fire on the rebels in those bushes. Pin down as many as you can."

I led my men up the fifty feet of beach until we fell in behind Moody's men. Moody and the rebel commander, whom I recognized as the young hothead Jeremiah Chadwick, were cursing each other. Moody, in his peculiar Scottish lilt, shouted, "You shall have no

quarter, for you deserve no quarter! I will run you through myself!"
Jeremiah Chadwick was as foulmouthed as his older brother, Thomas,
whom I kept secured in front of me. The younger Chadwick taunted
Moody, claiming he would "push in front of the buzzards" to dine on
Tory corpses that evening. He also pledged to grant no quarter to any
surrendering and wounded Loyalists who might be left behind.

Meanwhile, Gillian's brigands, God bless them, had surprised me
by doing exactly what was required. They settled in behind a wagon
and tree trunk on the south end of the beach and began a steady
fire. The largest party of rebels was now taking fire from a second
side. The rebel firing became less frequent, and I saw a few of them
break ranks and flee up the road.

I shouted down the berm, "Mr. Moody, you shall have the
honor of charging the rebel position and driving these cowards
from the beach!"

Moody's drummer began beating. Moody shouted, "Sergeants,
take your men over the berm and lance the rebels. NOW!" The
Scotsman raced forward with his men. I watched the volunteers, with
their bayonets, fall upon the rebels. The rebels used their muskets as
staffs and resisted, but several were skewered. Others bolted.

Then, without orders, Gillian's men raced into the mêlée. The
insubordination was galling, but their spirit was admirable. I watched
two of Gillian's Negroes tussling in the middle of it all, bayonets and
arms casting about. In middle of the fray, I saw Jeremiah Chadwick
fall to his knees, clutching his midsection. Foulmouthed to the end, he
damned the Loyalists for our supposed treachery and damned his own
men for giving ground. Then, one of the picaroons lanced him from
behind, and he was done. Within a minute of his collapse, the rebels
broke and fled. Cheers went up from the loyal men.

I called for John. He came toward me. "Help our wounded men
to the barges, and then bring forth the dead with as much dignity
and military honor as these brave souls deserve. All other men are
to return to their stations prior to this battle. Convey this to all the
men. I shall go to the boats and report to Captain Heyden. Then I'll
supervise the loading of the livestock."

John did as ordered. Moody's men resumed their defensive line at
the head of the beach. Most of Gillian's men took after the livestock

that had scattered during the mêlée. But in between my men in the surf and Moody's men standing guard on the beach were two of Gillian's Negroes. Scoundrels to the end, I saw them rifle through the possessions of the dead rebels and rob the wounded. One of the Negroes pulled shoes right off the feet of a prisoner. Their conduct sickened me, but there was no time to discipline the brigands now. The sun was setting, and the day's principal objects—the rebel officers and the livestock—still needed to be secured.

Soon, the barges were loaded to capacity, and John and Worthly came up. This told me that everything we wanted was loaded. Captain Heyden fired one of his swivel guns as a signal to Moody, and Moody withdrew his men down the beach, passing Gillian's picaroons on their way. Moody's men came lumbering through the surf with their muskets held over their heads and were pulled into the barges within a few minutes.

I called to the small barge, "Ensign Moody, you have done fine work today. Make ready to sail!"

"Aye, but what about Mr. Gillian and the refugees, Lieutenant? They won't have strength to hold the rebels if they return. There are still livestock to be recovered."

"The brigands have their own vessels and will fend for themselves—as they have done for the last two years. I have conferred with Captain Heyden, and we both believe we must leave now. If Mr. Gillian has concerns with our departure, he shall discuss them with me or the captain this evening at Sandy Hook."

The winds were excellent, and we made Sandy Hook by nine o'clock. A preliminary inventory of the haul suggested it was indeed a successful day. In the final analysis, Moody—and even that rascal Gillian—had carried themselves with bravery and a common purpose.

"Ensign Moody," I called as we unloaded my barge, "*you* shall take *your* prisoners to the commissary." I would give the ensign the honor of registering the prisoners and having them credited as his captures. This would suit Moody's ambition and remind him that a true gentleman does not seek personal glory from battle.

Surprised by my generosity, Moody sputtered a thank-you and tipped his hat.

I tipped my hat. "And a good evening to you, Ensign. Safe travels home tomorrow."

I told Worthly and John to let the men dip into the apple spirits that we had carried back. With the day over, I started feeling the cramp in my calf muscle again. It had tightened up on the barge. With the excitement of battle long passed, the pain lodged in the forefront of my mind again.

On my way back to the lighthouse, I limped past the collection of hovels and tents that compose Refugeetown, the residence of the black men. It continues to grow and now holds nearly as many women and children as men. There would be an awful racket this evening when Gillian's Negroes returned with a cask of spirits, a few goats and whatever pilfered silver and brass trinkets they took. The African has proven himself to be a ferocious fighter when brute force and animal courage are all that is required. But what will happen after the war when, having bested a white man in combat, the black man must return to his natural servile state?

Then I thought about my own difficult position: twenty-four years old and "retired" from service. I'm drawing a half-pay pension that doesn't come close to supporting a family. My brokenhearted father was slowly dying in a dismal Manhattan boardinghouse; my sister and John were unable to provide a good living for themselves. And as of today, the family home was burned to the ground. My share of today's haul would be good and might pay father's room and board for another few months, but excursions are a dangerous and unsteady source of income. What would become of my family if I were captured again? What might the rebels do to me now that the blood and embers of Tinton Falls are on my hands?

This thought and the evening chill made me shiver. Fortunately, it was a short walk from the tents to the lighthouse keeper's cottage. Sam Leonard and Joe Throckmorton had a small pot of steaming cider waiting for me. That night, they gave me the good bed without making me draw a card.

JEREMIAH CHADWICK

Revolutionary Officer

The American Revolution brought a new generation of political and military leaders to the fore. In Monmouth County, more than 80 percent of the new leaders were from the yeoman class or lower; one-third did not even own sufficient property to vote before the war (voting was reserved for men who owned fifty or more acres of land). Most of these new leaders were fully committed to American independence but were equally committed to raising their personal wealth and status. Derided as crude bumpkins by more genteel Loyalist adversaries, these new leaders nonetheless found synergy between Revolutionary zeal and personal ambition. By war's end, many of these new leaders advanced into the ranks of the wealthiest men in their county, but other new leaders suffered greatly—losing homes, loved ones and sometimes even their own lives.

Jeremiah Chadwick was among this new group of Revolutionary leaders. In 1777, when the Monmouth militia reorganized, he was elected a lieutenant of the Tinton Falls militia; his older brother, Thomas, was elected captain. The Chadwick brothers received this honor even though they were land poor. Together, Thomas and Jeremiah Chadwick led the most active of the eight militia companies in Shrewsbury Township. Jeremiah Chadwick was also a shipmaster; he needed to purchase a substitute for his militia tours while at sea. In 1779, Jeremiah Chadwick was indicted for assault, suggesting that his zeal for the Revolutionary cause sometimes boiled over into lawless violence. Despite this stain on his reputation, Jeremiah Chadwick was elected by his *co-congregants as sideman at the Anglican Christ Church in Shrewsbury. It appears that the brothers were positioned for greater wealth and higher social status when Thomas took possession of a confiscated Loyalist estate in May 1779, and Jeremiah returned home from sea (presumably with a profitable cargo). Tragedy struck a few weeks later when Loyalist raiders attacked at Tinton Falls.*

W as it a gunshot that stirred me? I sat up in my bed and pushed the arms of my girl, Silence, off of me. She shifted herself within the blankets, groaning, "Jerry…let me sleep. My head hurts."

"Be quiet, girl," I whispered. The irony of this girl being named Silence is never lost on me. She's a fine lay and that rare girl who doesn't worry that the village hens say things about her. One day I might marry her. But now she needs to shut up and lay quiet. Was that really a gunshot or was my head just foggy from last night?

Last night was wild. I stayed too late with Thomas at the Blue Ball tavern, lavishing my sailors and sundry others with drink. When the tavern keep told me and Thomas to go home, I spent far too much on his last bottle of whiskey, which Silence and I drank before bedding down. Silence is a fallen Quaker girl, too willful for that cult's strict ways. She now swills liquor like a Dutchman at a horse race. Yes, my conduct was excessive, but we needed to celebrate my safe return from Martinique with a cargo of sugar and molasses. When sold at public auction in two weeks, I will finally have enough money to purchase this cabin and the old Okerson mansion that Thomas is now occupying. Thomas and I have agreed that he will manage the mansion and its farm. With four sons and a good slave, he has the labor secured. I will get one-third of the crop revenues for five years in exchange for my investment. With this coin in my pocket, I will buy a large-berthed brig and, after a couple of good hauls, a row house among the gentlemen in Philadelphia. As a boy, I grew up sleeping on a thin blanket on a hardwood floor with Thomas and my three other brothers. We crowded together on winter nights to keep from freezing. Now, I am only six months from having real wealth and a fine home in the city. I'm within an ace of a dream come true. Perhaps that gunshot was just a dream, too?

I slid out of the blanket, pulled on my trousers and stepped into the main room of the cabin. The air was still chilled by the night despite the morning sun being up for perhaps an hour. All was quiet. "That was no gun. Last night's spirits have deceived me," I thought. But my reassurances didn't convince me. I took my musket and exited the cabin, stepping into the small yard. I scanned across Eaton's Creek toward town and looked at the Okerson mansion.

"Christ himself be damned. Redcoats!"

I ran back into the house. "Wake yourself, girl. We are in great danger. Everything is in great danger." Silence put a pillow over her head and rolled over. I grabbed her by the hair and pulled her within an inch of my face. "Wake now, stupid girl. This is not a game." Her eyes opened wide with fear.

"Saddle the horse. Then bring everything of value into the cabin. Do it now!"

I finished dressing, tearing my stocking as I pulled it up too rapidly. I went to my little sideboard and grabbed the box of musket balls that sat underneath it. My hands trembled as I scooped the balls into a sack. Nearly half of them tumbled onto the floor and rolled toward the south wall of the cabin and into the hearth. "God damn you, Dutchman!" I cursed Aucke Wikoff. He had the gall to tell me the cottage floor was level when I rented it from him. With no time to fish the errant balls out of the smoking hearth, I grabbed the half-filled sack and a second sack of powder and slung both across my back. Then I grabbed my musket and the rusty short sword that I had won in a dice game in Martinique. I kicked the door open and ran for the horse; Silence had just cinched up the saddle.

"Secure everything you can inside the cabin and then bar the door and stay inside. This will be a very hot day, and I need you safe."

I hoisted myself on my mare, Pandora, and headed down the narrow path for the road.

Hitting the Falls Road, I took a quick look up the road toward town and saw another party of Tories at Major Van Brunt's house. They were probably all about town. I turned south, heading away from them. My nephews told stories about my bravery, but there would be nothing brave about riding headlong into the Tories by myself—that would be suicide.

I needed to rally the men. The cannon that we used to signal alarms was behind Colonel Hendrickson's barn on the north side of town. There was no way to get there. I would need to go house to house. Fortunately, most of my men lived south of town. The first farm heading south belonged to the Bennetts. Theophillus Bennett was in his late fifties and claimed gout on militia days. His two grown boys—Abraham and Joel—missed as many militia tours as they made and never stopped fooling around and backbiting the officers when they did show up. I would be wasting my time to expect any patriotism from the likes of them at this dangerous moment. I galloped past their farmstead without calling out.

I would have better luck at the Holmes farmstead, only two stone's throws up the road. Jacob Holmes was from one of the largest families in the county, and nearly all of the Holmeses were strong supporters of the Continent. I shouted, "Jake Holmes, alarm! I am calling alarm!" Pandora carried me up their short driveway. Holmes and three of his boys came hustling out of the barn.

"Redcoats, at least a few dozen of them, maybe more, are at the Falls. You must gather your things and help me rally the militia. There is no time to waste."

Holmes dispatched his youngest boy to prepare his horse. He and his two sons, Amos and Sam, ran for their guns. "We must get more men—the entire platoon. Jacob, I need you to ride for Eatontown and rally everyone you can. Boys, you run up and down the road alerting all the families. I am going to the Blue Ball tavern to rouse my sailors and will dispatch riders for Colts Neck and Middletown. We will meet back here in one hour. You cannot fail."

An hour later, perhaps 9:00 a.m., I looked over the collection of men and boys who had answered their country's dire alarm. The turnout was damn disappointing. The raid six weeks earlier had made many of the farmers afraid to leave their farms. Others were just disaffected dogs who secretly wished harm on their new country. They will pay for their treason, even if I have to personally beat each one of their pasty hides myself.

About twenty Patriots, including Thomas's oldest sons, Jacob and Samuel, and three other boys not yet adults, were all that turned out for their country's defense. Only one of the company's sergeants—the tanner and shoemaker John Hayes—was present. Jacob Holmes reported his conversation with Captain Wainwright, who was rallying his company at Eatontown. Wainwright promised to come to the Falls by noon. But by then, the town might be nothing—just naked chimneys and cinders.

We were a ragged lot, middling farmers and sailors pulled from our plows and boats. Only half the men had good muskets; others had old blunderbusses that could not be relied on to shoot straight. A few had only axes or pitchforks. We were cut off from our magazine in Colonel Hendrickson's barn and would have to make do with whatever we had at this moment.

"Men, we are not numerous, and we are not well armed, but we are spirited by love of our town and country, and we are one thousand times braver than any Tory or British dog. We will head into town and attack the enemy. If they form up and prove themselves too numerous, you shall have permission to break ranks—but only on my order." I pointed to a sailor with an axe, barely fifteen from the looks of him, and two farm boys armed with only pitchforks. "You boys shall form into a line with us. Point your wood handles toward the enemy. From a distance, even a broomstick appears to be a fine musket."

"Sergeant Hayes, march the men forward."

Hayes called, "March on my three count. Today you are soldiers." And the men went forward. My huzzahs and cheers to the men fell on deaf ears. We all understood we could not stand against a well-formed enemy. But if we could pick off a few of their stragglers and bandits, we could keep them in close formation and limit their plundering. A few dead will make the cowards retreat early. Just two weeks ago, Colonel Holmes, with only sixty men, turned back two hundred Tories near Middletown. He bloodied the advance guard, and their timorous commander turned the whole party around. The mongrel Tory, whatever his advantages in numbers and arms, has no stomach for a real fight.

I left my horse in Holmes's barn and went off with my men. We trotted toward town behind Hayes. The pious men among us—Baptists mostly—sang a hymn about God's righteousness. I ran back and forth among the men, backslapping as we went and distributing extra cartridges to those who needed them. My hands trembled as I placed them into the men's hands, but I don't think anyone noticed.

We came up the Falls Road and saw two fires in the distance; later, we learned that they were at the home of Aucke Wikoff and the barn of Colonel Hendrickson. Worst was the fire at the new home of my brother, Thomas—the house that sat at the center of my plan to become a gentleman shipowner in Philadelphia. The infernal Tory, so blinded by his lust for revenge that he could commit the most wanton and senseless act, had fired the old Okerson mansion simply because it had been let out to a good family. I worried for my nephews and nieces. My anger built inside. "By damn, I will drink the blood of the man who put a torch to that house," I said to myself but loud enough for my men to hear.

In front of us, a party of ten red- and green-coated Tories loaded a wagon filled with my brother's furniture. Drunk with plunder, they didn't even notice as we came within eighty yards.

I motioned for the men to form up, and they stretched out fifty feet in a line in front of Eaton's Brook. I lowered my sword, and the men fired a volley at the Tories. One fell. The rest scurried off like frightened rabbits. A few men cheered, but I quieted them. "Nothing has happened yet, men. Reload. They will be coming back very soon."

Indeed, it took only five minutes for a line of maybe forty Tories, with a handful of robbers on each flank, to come out of town toward to us. The beating of a military drum told as us that the Tories were forming up for an advance even as the smoke blurred our view. My men reloaded, and we readied to put shot amongst them. "Steady boys, hold yer fire. Hold yer fire. Wait for my signal."

A hundred feet away, down near the bridge, a woman and a girl came running through the smoke. "Hold yer fire!" Hayes yelled, and the woman passed through the far end of the line. It all happened so quickly that I thought my eyes deceived me, so I looked again. It was Elizabeth and Sarah, Thomas's wife and daughter, fleeing from their persecutors. I wanted to go to them, but if I broke ranks, my men would, too. All would be lost. I refocused on the enemy.

The Tories fanned out in a line as they came toward us. "Steady. Steady, steady," I cautioned.

When they came within fifty yards, their officer called, "Make ready!" I shouted, "Now men, hit them!"

The men offered the Tories their best volley, and we hit another one of them. Then came their reply; five feet from me, a ball lodged in a sailor's neck. He gagged horribly and fell. Another ball hit Jacob Holmes in the leg.

The Tory officer called for the men to advance. Damn my ears and eyes! The officer's womanly voice and long hair were familiar. Their officer was Thomas Okerson, a damned fool of a dandy and the eldest son of old man Okerson, the Tory who once owned Thomas's new house. Okerson had fired his father's own house, the house of his childhood, rather than let my brother's family live there peacefully. I would find special pleasure in killing him.

On Okerson's call, the Tories charged us. My men broke and fled before the Tories even reached the brook; I had no choice but to take off with them.

We ran all the way back to Holmes's house. I was winded and angry that my men broke without my permission. But we were outnumbered and lacked the bayonets to fight them hand-to-hand. I looked at the sullen faces of the sailors and farmers around me. "Chin up, my boys. Revenge will come later today. The country is now alarmed. With each minute the enemy stays, the balance tips a little more in our favor."

There was little to do now but post a sentry in our rear and wait. I sent young Amos Holmes to spy at the edges of town. He came back an hour later with intelligence that Tory parties had broken into the homes of all the principal men and had taken Colonels Hendrickson and Wikoff, Major Van Brunt and my brother. The prisoners sat captured in a heavily guarded wagon.

I thought about Thomas and his sons, Jacob and Samuel, with me now. I thought about Silence and whether I could stand the scandal that would arise if I married such a fallen woman. I thought about my ship's cargo, safely deposited at Toms River, and the price it would fetch at auction. I thought about how today had so thoroughly disrupted my plans to amass a fortune and achieve gentility.

If assistance came from the south, it would be from Wainwright's Eatontown militiamen or the Shrewsbury men under Captain Hampton. But both companies were plagued with disaffection. How many of these men might answer the alarm and risk their lives for Tinton Falls was an open question. To the west, the militia was more reliable. The Middletown men of Captain Smock and the wild-eyed Colts Neck men of Captain Green were surely alarmed by now and on their way. However, the Tories occupied the village in between my position and the western approaches these militia would use. I was cut off from them.

And so we waited for Wainwright and Hampton in Holmes's yard. For the next three hours, the men bided time rolling cartridges until we ran out of balls—of which he had far too few. Mostly, the men lay idle in Holmes's yard. Three country boys came in, as did the Jewish peddler, Levi Hart, who let the men put their dippers into his small barrel of apple spirits. He also sold me his two small pouches of musket balls at a very moderate price. Hart pulled his wagon behind Holmes's house and then came forward with a curved dagger, which he said was from Africa, and a rifle, an exotic weapon in eastern in New Jersey.

"The finest rifle in this county will strike down our most hateful enemy today, Lieutenant." Hart's arrival and his apple spirits cheered my men a little; he was not from our district, and I could not have compelled him to serve with us. Still, even with Hart and a few stragglers increasing our numbers, we waited for reinforcement.

Finally, about 1:00 p.m., the sentry called, "The militia are a-coming up the road!"

"Cheer up, lads. Now we shall free the Falls and send the Tories to hell." I rushed down onto the road to greet the reinforcements, with several of my men, now cheering, in close pursuit.

My disappointment must have been palpable. Indeed, Captains Wainwright and Hampton had rallied to Tinton Falls' assistance— but with only twenty men among them in their rear. Wainwright, like myself an officer at the Christ Church in Shrewsbury, motioned for me to come forward. We walked off into a cornfield to speak privately. "I am so sorry, Jeremiah. The men of my district are very backward. On my alarm, they secret themselves in their lofts and cellars or flee into the woods. Half of them probably side with the Tories, and the other half are from families that have already suffered greatly. They are afraid they will be burnt out of their houses next week for marching with me today." He looked at the smoke plumes. "God have mercy on the good people of Tinton Falls. How bad is it?"

"The Tories are in town. They have razed the plantations of Hendrickson and Wikoff. They've also razed Thomas's new home, the old Okerson estate. They are led by no less than Thomas Okerson—who has fired his own childhood home rather than see a good family possess it. They have my brother. And I watched his wife and my little niece rush past me like frightened mice after the barbarians put torch to the mansion. I drew up the men and attacked. We stood them for a few minutes at Eaton's Creek, hitting two of theirs and taking wounds to two of ours. But they are too well armed and too numerous. So we fell back."

Captain Hampton came to us. "I left my Lieutenant, Dan Hullets, in Shrewsbury to press more men. I am told that the enemy's barges are lying at Jumping Point, so Hulletts will meet us near there with whomever he can summon. I have also sent my best riders to Captains Green and Smock telling them where the enemy barges lay." Hampton, ever the pragmatic shopkeeper, had already determined that the Falls could not be rescued and that the enemy could only be effectively attacked on its retreat to its barges. I repressed an urge to strangle this man who so cavalierly calculated that my town was beyond hope. My cheeks flushed. "Curse you, Hampton, for giving up the best village in all of East Jersey. I will—"

Wainwright put his hand on my shoulder and calmly spoke over me. "I am so sad for you, Jeremiah, but Captain Hampton is right. We cannot dislodge the enemy from the Falls, but we can harass them if they overextend and pick off any straggling parties. We will harass their rear and flanks until they are on their boats. With any luck, we will get a clean shot at Okerson, and I will offer my best bullock to any man who brings him down." He leaned in close and whispered, "Focus your temper on our enemy, my friend. Not on the man who risks his life to fight at your side when his home faces no danger."

Wainwright managed to quell my anger, just as he had often done at our church vestry meetings. I offered my hand to Captain Hampton. "My anger is my demon, Captain. But it is now your obedient servant."

Hampton's hand covered mine. "Your anger is less your demon than the Tory is a demon to our country, Lieutenant. When we defeat the Tories this afternoon, you shall have the honor of accepting their officer's surrender." I nodded to the captain for his generous sentiments. But I didn't express my own: if Okerson surrendered to me, I would gut him with my sword. And if Hampton or another of the so-called due process men brought me up on charges for slaying such a villain, then damn them, too. No jury would dare convict me.

As the senior officer amongst us, my men fell in under Hampton. The captain was good to his word. He and Wainwright split the militia—fifty-four of us in all—and each took command of half. Both parties pinched in at the edges of the Falls and skirmished with their pickets. With the captain's approval, I led a ten-man party in chasing off a half dozen robbers plundering the Yates farm just a quarter mile from my cabin. Perhaps because of the pressure we were putting on the Tory foragers, they collapsed back toward town.

In an hour, the Tories formed up and marched out of town toward the shore, but we continued to take shots and spread mayhem amongst them. This panicked their stolen livestock and slowed their descent. Up the road ahead of us, I caught glimpses of Wainwright's party, in clusters of six or eight, confronting the Tories. The Eatontown militia took a few shots and scattered before the mounted Tories approached. Meanwhile, Hampton and I kept a running fire on the Tory rear guard.

A mile into our pursuit, we were joined by Captain Smock's fifty Middletown men, greatly raising our spirits. We now achieved parity with the enemy. As the running fire continued, we continued to grow. Hulletts arrived from Shrewsbury with fifteen more men; a dozen of the new state troops met us at Hartshorne's abandoned plantation. These boys were green, but they came with full complements of cartridges. Eight men from inside the village of Tinton Falls—reduced to hiding in their cellars hours earlier—formed up under Lieutenant Aucke Hendrickson, son of our captured colonel. They came running out to us. Hendrickson and I embraced and wept briefly together over the fate of our kinsmen. The men cheered as we swore revenge.

But even as our strength increased, the Tories remained formidable. Twice, their mounted party—armed with sabers and pistols—rode down into us. On one of their descents, a Tory opened up the shoulder of young Tunis Vanderveer of Middletown, who had to be carried off the road and left in a stand of trees. We shot the horse out from under one of their men.

We pressed the Tories all the way to the beach at Jumping Point. The sky darkened. Thunder and gunfire made the animals jumpy. It was almost comical watching the Tories wading into the water, pulling stubborn goats with ropes and tackling loose pigs. They had a gunboat amongst their barges, but it kept silent. A single cannon shot would have panicked the beasts completely.

Hampton pointed the militia detachments toward different spots on the edge of the beach, mostly clusters of bushes and thickets. A line of fifty Tories drew up on the beach to protect their motley animal tamers. As directed, I led my men to a patch of meadow grass and scraggly cypress trees at the top of the beach. Firing began on both sides, but we were too far from the Tories to do any damage. For twenty minutes, I watched this ineffectual skirmish; my shouts to Hampton to press in on the Tories went unheeded. Beyond the reach of our pointless skirmishing, Tories continued to load their plunder, plunder stolen from the families of Tinton Falls.

I ran to a nearby hedge of scrub to confer with Lieutenant Hendrickson. "Aukey, this is madness. We fire at them, and they fire back at us. Our balls fall harmlessly one in front of the other. Your father will soon be lost, as will my brother. I will lead an assault on the Tory line; you must follow."

He nodded gravely. "Some will call this insubordination, Jeremiah. But yes, I will follow with my men."

I ran back to my men. "Boys. On my charge, we head for the sand berm in front of the Tory line. They will taste our metal from close in. Hart, load your fine rifle now. I will call out the officer, and you will strike him down." I called, "Now! Volunteers of Tinton Falls, forward!" And we sprinted up a hundred feet and then crashed behind the sand berm without taking a loss. Hendrickson's small group landed on the berm a minute later.

In close and loaded, we fired a deadly volley that hit three Tories. The Tories fired back, but we were secure behind the berm. I poked my head over and looked for Okerson but could not find him. I shouted across to the Tories, "I am Jeremiah Chadwick. You have taken my brother, run off his family and burned his house. I shall avenge him! I will kill each of you, dismember your bodies and cast your limbs into the surf. Bring forward that coward Okerson who tortures women and children and release the prisoners and livestock. Then I will let you go off."

An officer with a Scottish accent called back, "You will find nothing but lead from my gun in your bowels and my sword in your skull. Pull back now, rebel!" The shouts between me and the Scotsman continued.

Behind the Scotsman's line, I saw Okerson talking to one of his men. "Hart, come stand next to me. Lower your rifle on Okerson. There he is—the man in the fancy cocked hat thinking he is Sir Henry Clinton." Hart came forward and leveled the gun. "I will fire, Jeremiah, on your order. But there are men in front of Okerson. I think they are our men, I might hit one of ours."

Indeed, they were ours. Okerson had put five blindfolded prisoners, tied together at their feet judging by their shambling, in front of him. Hart and I watched Okerson move back and forth. By God, his prisoners moved with him—always in front of him. From a distance, it was hard to tell, but it looked like Okerson was using Tinton Falls' best men—Colonel Hendrickson, Lieutenant Colonel Wikoff, Major Van Brunt, Captain McKnight and my own brother, Thomas—as human shields. My hands shook at the treachery.

Another line of Tories rushed forward behind the Scotsman. We continued to fire into them. "Damn you and your Tory treachery! You'll roast in hell for using prisoners to protect your officers. But even the devil will show you more mercy than I will. Do not call for quarter; you will receive nothing but my sword."

The firing and shouts continued, but several of my men were now dangerously low on ammunition; a few were out. Some of the men asked for permission to fall back. I exhorted them, "Stay in tight, men. They cannot beat us if we stay together. Stay in tight."

Then the Tories, led by the Scotsman, came forward with bayonets pointing at us. I stood over the berm and shouted, "Over the berm, men! Meet them on the high ground." I went over with my sword in front, but only half of my men followed.

The Tories closed in. At twenty feet, the Scotsman leveled his pistol at me and fired. I felt a hideous burning sensation in my belly and was conscious of some more of my men pulling back. The land under my feet started swirling, swallowing my feet. "Damn the Tories, and damn the cowards of Tinton Falls who retreat at this critical moment! Damn you all. I will send you all to the Devil myself!" I was aware of fighting all around me. There were shouts. Bells rang in my ears. My bowels burned.

I thrust my arm forward to stab at the Scotsman, but the sword was gone from my hand. The lunge raised the burning in my stomach. My hands dropped to cradle the guts that now poured out of me.

"Scotsman, I will take your ball and cram it up your arse. Face me, Scotsman."

But the ground was now swirling faster, and my feet failed to move me. My eyes blurred, and my legs buckled. I was on my knees. Tears came from my eyes. "Forgive me, Lord, for my intemperance. Thomas, you must avenge me!"

There was a searing pain in my back and then through my chest in front. I looked down to see a blade emerging out of my chest with dark purple matter on its end. The swirling ground raced forward, encompassing my face. Dirt filled my mouth. I coughed and trembled.

I was riding Pandora to safety. I was on a light blue sea bringing home a cargo of rum on a brisk northerly wind. I was at the

Blue Ball tavern with Thomas, laughing about the war bringing us such good fortune. Raindrops patted the back of my head. The ringing in my ears deafened me. My body burned incredibly. Then all was black.

POSTSCRIPT

Tinton Falls was vulnerable to attack in June 1779 because the Continental army had recently withdrawn from the area, the local militia was ineffective and the newly established state troops were not yet ready for combat. The June 10 raid signaled a new kind of warfare in Monmouth County. Prior raids had military aims. For example, the April 25 raid six weeks earlier was supposed to capture a Continental army regiment. But the main purpose of the June 10 raid was to punish the village of Tinton Falls, particularly its Revolutionary leaders, for past abuses against Loyalists.

The vindictive nature of the June 10 raid was not lost on the people of northeastern Monmouth County. After the April 25 raid, the Revolutionaries of Tinton Falls continued with life as before, but they could not return to normal after June 10.

In the days following the June 10 raid, many families loyal to the Revolutionary government fled inland for safety; others made plans to do so. Hoping to reverse the trend, New Jersey governor William Livingston dispatched Robert Morris, the chief justice of the New Jersey Supreme Court, to Tinton Falls to rally the people. After a few days at Tinton Falls, the chief justice reported that nearly all the livestock in the area was gone, and the locals were desperate: "Some are quitting their habitations, and others declare they are willing to do so, observing that if they must go on starving, they had rather do it in the country than in the [British] Provost Jail." Morris was pessimistic that he could maintain the local militia now that its senior officers were kidnapped: "[I] have got them to embody…but as they are but farmers and mechanics in but middling circumstances, I have little hopes of continuing it long."

There are no surviving records of the families who fled Tinton Falls after the raid, but a list compiled by Captain James Green of Colts Neck in 1780 documents that fifteen women from the Tinton Falls area—including formerly prosperous Deborah Williams—were still under the care of the Colts Neck militia thirteen months after the raid. New Jersey's main newspaper, the *New Jersey Gazette*, and Philadelphia newspapers advertised several estate sales along the Monmouth shore in the months following the raid.

The traumatic impact of the raid is further evidenced by examining the post-raid lives of the five village leaders kidnapped on June 10. All five—Lieutenant Colonel Aucke Wikoff, Colonel Daniel Hendrickson, Major Hendrick Van Brunt, Captain Richard McKnight and Captain Thomas Chadwick—suffered reversals of fortune afterward. Aucke Wikoff received harsh treatment from his captors. He was kept in jail even as other officers were paroled home around him. Even after fifteen months in confinement, Wikoff's parole was denied—probably because he was so despised by the Loyalists. Wikoff eventually returned home but was never again active in local government or the militia, suggesting ill health and a loss of stature in the community. His last slave ran off while he was confined.

Daniel Hendrickson helped arrange his own prisoner exchange in December 1779 and resumed command of the local militia. But the six months in jail and destruction of his property apparently radicalized him. Upon his release, he became involved in a vigilante group known as the Retaliators. He was implicated in a string of scandals—including twice participating in election day voter intimidation. He was also reprimanded by the governor for ignoring orders. Hendrickson was elected to the state legislature in a rigged election in 1785, but the state intervened and overturned the results. He moved west of the Appalachians a few years later and never returned.

After several months in jail, Hendrick Van Brunt came home. But he was captured a second time in September 1780 and retired from public life after his second release. Richard McKnight was released from confinement in 1780 and retired from service, probably due to illness. He died in 1782.

Of the five Tinton Falls leaders kidnapped on June 10, 1779, only Thomas Chadwick distinguished himself as a local leader after the raid. He resumed command of his militia company in late 1779 and led the militia in at least two engagements against the Loyalists. Never a wealthy man, he finally acquired the means to purchase a confiscated Loyalist estate at auction in 1784—only to die shortly thereafter.

For the Loyalists who led the June 10 raid against Tinton Falls, the raid represented a high point in their careers. Thomas Okerson remained an active Loyalist raider through the end of the war, even after rejoining the army in 1781. But there is no evidence that he led any other equally successful raids. In 1782, Okerson brought a small party of Loyalists back into Monmouth County, but he and his brother were captured in that engagement.

James Moody continued as an active Loyalist through the end of the war, as well. Moody became infamous throughout New Jersey for his many bold descents on Continental army and congressional mail carriers. But for all his activity, Moody never again equaled the success of the June 10, 1779 raid. After the war, Moody went to England and wrote a popular, self-aggrandizing autobiography about his wartime exploits.

William Gillian continued to assault Monmouth County after the Tinton Falls raid. He led at least two other raids into Monmouth County (one resulting in a murder of an old man; the other resulting in the capture of a militia lieutenant), but none of his actions were on par with the June 10 raid. Gillian disappears from the historical record after 1781.

Chrineyonce Van Mater also remained an active Loyalist after the June 10 raid. But in 1780, he was captured after landing in Monmouth County with two trunks of counterfeit Continental currency. In 1782, Van Mater was tried for high treason but was apparently found not guilty. He was one of only a few prominent

Monmouth County Loyalists who resettled in the county after the war. In 1784, he was residing in Middletown with 226 acres, ten livestock and a slave—a comfortable farm but modest in comparison to his family's prewar estates.

For the African American Loyalists on Sandy Hook, their best days were ahead. In 1780, they confederated into a group known as the "Black Brigade," which launched several successful raids into Monmouth County, three of which were similar in size and impact to the June 10, 1779 raid. Under the leadership of a runaway slave named Titus (nicknamed Colonel Tye), the African American Loyalists attacked Monmouth County three times in June 1780 alone and carried off two legislators and the lieutenant colonel of the Middletown militia. The Black Brigade grew increasingly bold as the summer went on, moving farther inland. It struck Colts Neck twice and plundered at the edge of Freehold—the well-guarded, inland county seat. Among its additional captures were two militia captains, James Green and Joshua Huddy, and Major Hendrick Van Brunt (his second time taken).

But the heyday of the Black Brigade was short. Colonel Tye was wounded in a skirmish in September 1780 and died days later. Shortly after that, a party of African American raiders was slaughtered at Long Branch (the so-called Negro Hill Massacre). In 1781, the Black Brigade dissolved as a cohesive military unit. African American Loyalists stayed active through the end of the war, but they returned to raiding under white leaders. In their last major recorded action, forty African American raiders came together with forty white raiders under Captain Davenport in a June 1782 descent on Forked River. But they scattered in a panic when a militia party surprised them and shot Davenport at close range. In April 1783, forty-nine men, twenty-three women and six children, the remnants of the Black Brigade, were boarded on the *L'Abondance* and resettled in Canada.

When the Continentals left eastern Monmouth County in May 1779, they never returned. However, the county militia improved markedly in 1780 when officers started aggressively fining men for delinquency and beacons were constructed to quickly communicate alarms. Starting in 1780 and continuing through the end of the war, the state troops maintained an effective fighting strength of 200 to 300 men under the competent command of Colonel Asher Holmes. While they lost as many engagements as they won, the state troops never again turned away from a fight. When a massive Loyalist raiding party of 1,500 men attacked Middletown in June 1781, the state troops and militia did not have the strength to defeat it, but they did not scatter. They maintained a disciplined fire on the raiders' flanks all day, harassing them and minimizing the plundering.

It is unclear exactly when the Revolutionaries of Tinton Falls returned home, but fragmentary evidence suggests that they were gone for at least a year. In 1782, taxes were again collected, proving that the village had returned to some level of normalcy. But the tax collector needed to be accompanied by an armed guard. Normalcy was relative in this still-vulnerable region. A comparison of the tax rolls of 1779 and 1784 indicates that far more families dropped in wealth than gained in wealth in that time period.

In April 1782, a refugee party under Richard Lippincott, formerly of Shrewsbury, crossed into Monmouth County and hanged Captain Joshua Huddy of Colts Neck. Huddy's hanging was an act of retaliation for the murder of Shrewsbury Loyalist Philip White a few weeks earlier. After Huddy's hanging, General Washington demanded Lippincott and threatened to hang a British officer if Lippincott were not produced. The so-called Huddy Affair escalated into a diplomatic bonfire. The brutal little war around Monmouth County was now complicating the Paris peace negotiations.

In response, the new British commander in chief in America, General Guy Carleton, banned any further raiding. Six months after the Battle of Yorktown supposedly ended hostilities, the British finally reined in their Loyalist allies. Loyalist evacuations to Canada began a few months later and were completed by the end of 1783. Only when the British and Loyalists finally left Sandy Hook in January 1784 could the families of Tinton Falls feel secure again.

Appendix

FACT, FICTION AND
CONJECTURE IN
THE RAZING OF TINTON FALLS

All through the drafting of The Razing of Tinton Falls *I worried that the book might mislead readers. So much historical fiction overdramatizes and romanticizes the historical events that are portrayed. I wanted to write a book in the best tradition of narrative nonfiction; one that would adhere closely to historical fact even while recognizing that gaps in the historical record would require some fictionalization.*

As I drafted the book, I realized that the holes in the historical record were larger than I first anticipated. Completing the ten narratives required me to take more liberties than I first thought would be necessary. Feedback from test readers pushed me to take additional liberties as I responded to comments and amended the manuscript to create a more engaging book. As I started taking liberties from known fact, I determined to balance this trend with an essay that would help readers understand the boundaries of fact and fiction in this book and better ground the increasingly fictionalized manuscript in the narrative nonfiction genre. That essay is below.

O f all the raids and skirmishes to occur in Monmouth County during the American Revolution, over one hundred in total, the raid of June 10, 1779, is among the best documented.

Especially informative are three narratives written by people close to the event. One of the Loyalist co-leaders of the Tinton Falls raid, James Moody, wrote an autobiography of his Revolutionary War exploits. The book includes a detailed, if self-aggrandizing, narrative of the raid. The storekeeper at Tinton Falls, Benjamin White, also wrote an autobiography that discussed the raid and its impact on the village. A young daughter of Captain Thomas Chadwick, Eliza, heard her parents' stories of the raid and recorded them as an adult.

In addition to these accounts, the June 10, 1779 raid was documented in newspaper reports appearing in the *New Jersey Gazette*, the *New York Gazette & Weekly Mercury* and the *New York Royal Gazette*. Each of these reports differs in important ways. For example, different men are reported as commanding the Loyalists during the raid. New Jersey chief justice Robert Morris's letters from Tinton Falls discuss the raid's aftermath. A handful of other documents discuss the raid, including two Revolutionary War veterans' pension narratives and several antiquarian local history sources.

Other documents provide the context necessary for understanding the events of June 10, 1779. Military papers at the New Jersey State Archives offer details on the local militia and state troops before and after the raid. British military records in Great Britain's Public Record Office and the papers of British commander in chief General Henry Clinton provide information about the Loyalists who participated in the raid and the Loyalist camp at Sandy Hook. Finally, a receipt in the Henry Clinton papers conclusively documents the capture of the five senior militia officers from Tinton Falls, in addition to two privates.

Complementing these documents, I have spent more than twenty years assembling two large data sets about the American Revolution in Monmouth County: a six-thousand-entry activities database on war-related events and a seven-thousand-entry biographical file on the people who lived there. These data sets made it possible to build realistic biographies around the ten real people selected as narrators in *The Razing of Tinton Falls*.

This information was further refined by a set of experts—Todd Braisted, John Fabiano, David Fowler, Don Hagist and Bernadette

Rogoff—who peer-reviewed the near-final manuscript and provided helpful technical corrections on a range of topics, including the biographies of the ten narrators, Revolutionary War military convention and material culture. All told, a great commitment was made to write *The Razing of Tinton Falls* as a book well grounded in known fact.

Nonetheless, the details in each of the book's ten narratives are a collection of fact, conjecture informed by fact and outright fiction. There are simply too many holes in the historical record to write this book without fictionalization. In some of the narratives, documentation was so slight that the narrative had to be largely imagined.

I want readers to understand the boundaries between fact and fiction in this book. Below is a discussion of the limits of fact in *The Razing of Tinton Falls*.

GENEALOGICAL LIMITATIONS

Genealogical information for the ten narrators is scattered and incomplete. While I made a good-faith attempt to familiarize myself with genealogical information on key people in the book, the research was not exhaustive and was limited by significant gaps. For example, to the best of my knowledge, there is no genealogic record for two of the narrators, Sip and Esther Headon. Some families that are prominent in the book—like the Chadwicks and Taylors—have considerable genealogical documentation, but the strict application of that information to the corresponding narratives was difficult. For example, most colonial families were very large, but including all siblings in the narratives confused test readers. Family members were removed from later drafts of the book.

Certain names were frustratingly common in Revolutionary Monmouth County, and this complicated the accuracy of the narratives. For example, it is known that a young woman named Mary Taylor married a Continental soldier, John Hagerty of Virginia, while Hagerty was stationed at Tinton Falls. However, it cannot be proven that the Mary Taylor who married Hagerty was the same Mary Taylor who was the daughter of Loyalist leader George Taylor (though George Taylor owned a farm near Tinton Falls). Additional complications arose when different genealogical sources offered conflicting information about the same person. Different Williams family genealogies, for example, suggest different facts for Deborah Williams. Finally, a few pieces of known genealogical information were deliberately excluded from the narrative in the interest of facilitating a more coherent and interesting book.

Knowing that readers with genealogical interests will be concerned with the family details presented in this book, I offer a strong caution: In all cases, the familial descriptions and relationships described in the ten narratives should be regarded as fictional. Some factual genealogical details are offered in the chapter introductions.

WORD CHOICE AND DIALOGUE

Eighteenth-century dialogue and writing include non-intuitive contractions and abbreviations (i.e. Jno for John) and archaic words (i.e., hither, 'tis) that would not be well understood by the typical twenty-first-century reader. Archaic terms are not used in this book. In addition, eighteenth-century Americans employed terms that are unrecognizable to most twenty-first-century American readers. For example, supporters of the Revolution did not call themselves Patriots or Revolutionaries (the term used in this book). Most often, they called themselves "Whigs"—a term that tied them to the party of political reform in the British Parliament. In general, I opted to change out difficult eighteenth-century terminology for twenty-first-century terminology.

Eighteenth-century English was also spoken (and written) with qualifying and deferential language that confounds the twenty-first-century American ear. I chose to structure sentences and paragraphs to fit twenty-first-century norms, even though this lessens the book's historical accuracy. Further, in Revolutionary Monmouth County, many of the residents spoke Dutch as their primary language. (The records of the Dutch Reformed Church at Marlboro were kept in Dutch, not English, into the 1780s.) Early drafts of *The Razing of Tinton Falls* included many direct quotes from Revolutionary-era documents and some Dutch words. But the authentic language confused test readers and was therefore pared back during the editing process. Some authentic phrases from Monmouth County documents—i.e., "a friend to everyone in the world," "now the staff is in our hands," "they behaved like wild or mad men," "your bow has two strings," "grease the rope and tie the knot"—were maintained, but there are far fewer than in the early drafts.

LOCATIONS, PERSONAL APPEARANCE AND MATERIAL CULTURE

While great effort was made to compile details on the people and places detailed in *The Razing of Tinton Falls*, gaps in the historical record made guesswork necessary. Details of the layout of Tinton Falls, the landing points of the Loyalist raiders, local roads and other topographical features are informed by historical documents but are nonetheless largely fictional. In a few cases, such as the naming of Eaton's Creek just south of the village, landmarks were invented so that readers could better recognize common events across the narratives.

Similarly, nearly all of the physical descriptions of the people in the book are fictional. The historical record simply does not include their portraits or descriptions. In a few cases, known facts were deliberately changed—as in the case of James Moody, who was made a Scottish-accented immigrant so he'd be recognizable across chapters. With regard to the accuracy of descriptions of homes and personal goods, I relied on eighteenth-century estate inventories, merchant account books and surviving historic homes to ground the descriptions in historical fact. Nonetheless, the individual descriptions are fictional.

APPENDIX

NARRATOR SUBJECTIVITY

The narrators of each chapter differ greatly but are united in having biases about the events of June 10, 1779. Events are narrated from their viewpoints. For example, Benjamin White's depiction of Captain James Green and the Colts Neck militia is less sympathetic than Richard Laird's. The reader is expected to understand the subjectivity of the narrators and "read between the lines," understanding that each narrator is coloring events and selecting details to include or exclude. *The Razing of Tinton Falls* is as much a book about the subjectivity of truth as it is a book about a historical event.

BIASED AND INCOMPLETE SOURCES

The sources that inform this book are biased. Revolutionary War veterans' pension narratives, for example, were written by aging veterans eager to prove themselves long-serving and faithful Revolutionary soldiers and militiamen. These men had a vested interest in portraying themselves as spirited and unwavering supporters of the Revolution even when they were not. Similarly, James Moody wrote his autobiography while lobbying British authorities for a generous postwar stipend; he had a vested interest in exaggerating his role and minimizing the role of others. (Thomas Okerson is not even mentioned in Moody's autobiography.) Even the three newspaper accounts of the raid differ in key details: Loyalist leaders, casualty figures, the use of prisoners as human shields and Lieutenant Jeremiah Chadwick's reported refusal to grant quarter. I attempted to sift through these differences and select the "facts" that appear most plausible, but there is much room for contrasting interpretations.

There is less information concerning marginalized and poor people than leaders and wealthy people. Newspaper reports of military events, for example, nearly always list the names of officers and almost never list the names of privates (except when they are killed in action). As a result, particularly in discussing the Loyalist irregulars, there was a need to combine information on multiple people into a single person in the book (i.e., information on Moffit Taylor and Elisha Grooms was combined).

The narratives about women and poorer people involve more conjecture and imagination. For example, besides the record of her birth, there is no information about Sarah Chadwick in the historical record until her marriage in 1796. Similarly, while it is known that Sip participated in irregular Loyalist actions before and after the June 10, 1779 raid, it cannot be proven that he participated in the Tinton Falls raid. He is included in the book because African American Loyalists like Sip went unnamed in most Loyalist raids, and documentation of Sip's overall war record is better than most of the other black Loyalists who raided out of Sandy Hook.

Similarly, there is no hard evidence that the Hulse family participated in the skirmishing around Tinton Falls. This is plausible—even likely—but unproven. Less documentation meant more imagination in constructing the narrative. In all cases, the narratives are broadly consistent with life along the Monmouth County military frontier, but each of the narratives—particularly those involving poor and marginal people—required a good deal of imagination.

SCOPE OF THE BOOK

The narrow focus of the book—a raid that destroyed a village and depleted surrounding farms of their livestock—fosters a distortion. June 10, 1779, was indeed a terrible day for the people of Tinton Falls and many who lived near the village. But for people even a few miles away, it was not an exceptional day—particularly for those families who ignored the militia alarm. During the war, Monmouth County hosted over one hundred battles and skirmishes; nearly all of them were narrow events with little direct impact outside the enemy's line of march. Over the course of the war, a half dozen Monmouth County villages were razed, and the Tinton Falls experience of June 10, 1779, can be viewed as representative of that collective experience. But it is important to note the narrow scope of the raid.

The Esther Headon and Mary Taylor narratives are included in *The Razing of Tinton Falls* to remind readers that people could be impacted by the raid without being in the line of march; conversely, many people living close to Tinton Falls—through good luck or skillfully maintained neutrality—survived the day with minimal impact. Including the narrative of a person whose life was not impacted by the raid would have increased the historical accuracy of the book but made for dull reading.

In addition to the above, I discuss specific factual limitations of each of the book's ten narratives in a detailed essay that is posted on my website, www.michaeladelberg.com. However, even this in-depth examination cannot deconstruct every statement made in each narrative. When in doubt, readers are reminded that the ten narratives in *The Razing of Tinton Falls* are fictionalized accounts of a real event. While this book contains significant nonfiction text in chapter introductions, background and postscript sections, large parts of the narratives are fictional.

ABOUT THE AUTHOR

Michael Adelberg has been researching the American Revolution in Monmouth County for more than twenty years and is the author of the award-winning *The American Revolution in Monmouth County: The Theatre of Spoil and Destruction*. His essays on the American Revolution have appeared in scholarly journals like the *Journal of Military History* and the *Journal of the Early Republic*. He is a fiction reviewer for the *New York Journal of Books*, and his first novel, *A Thinking Man's Bully*, was published in January 2012. Adelberg holds master's degrees in history and public policy and lives with his family in Vienna, Virginia.

Visit us at
www.historypress.net